Strangers and Wayfarers

Strangers and Wayfarers

Sarah Orne Jewett

MINT EDITIONS

Strangers and Wayfarers was first published in 1890.

This edition published by Mint Editions 2021.

ISBN 9781513279879 | E-ISBN 9781513284897

Published by Mint Editions®

 MINT
EDITIONS

minteditionbooks.com

Publishing Director: Jennifer Newens
Design & Production: Rachel Lopez Metzger
Project Manager: Micaela Clark
Typesetting: Westchester Publishing Services

Contents

A WINTER COURTSHIP

The passenger and mail transportation between the towns of North Kilby and Sanscrit Pond was carried on by Mr. Jefferson Briley, whose two-seated covered wagon was usually much too large for the demands of business. Both the Sanscrit Pond and North Kilby people were stayers-at-home, and Mr. Briley often made his seven-mile journey in entire solitude, except for the limp leather mail-bag, which he held firmly to the floor of the carriage with his heavily shod left foot. The mail-bag had almost a personality to him, born of long association. Mr. Briley was a meek and timid-looking body, but he held a warlike soul, and encouraged his fancies by reading awful tales of bloodshed and lawlessness, in the far West. Mindful of stage robberies and train thieves, and of express messengers who died at their posts, he was prepared for anything; and although he had trusted to his own strength and bravery these many years, he carried a heavy pistol under his front-seat cushion for better defense. This awful weapon was familiar to all his regular passengers, and was usually shown to strangers by the time two of the seven miles of Mr. Briley's route had been passed. The pistol was not loaded. Nobody (at least not Mr. Briley himself) doubted that the mere sight of such a weapon would turn the boldest adventurer aside.

Protected by such a man and such a piece of armament, one gray Friday morning in the edge of winter, Mrs. Fanny Tobin was traveling from Sanscrit Pond to North Kilby. She was an elderly and feeble-looking woman, but with a shrewd twinkle in her eyes, and she felt very anxious about her numerous pieces of baggage and her own personal safety. She was enveloped in many shawls and smaller wrappings, but they were not securely fastened, and kept getting undone and flying loose, so that the bitter December cold seemed to be picking a lock now and then, and creeping in to steal away the little warmth she had. Mr. Briley was cold, too, and could only cheer himself by remembering the valor of those pony-express drivers of the pre-railroad days, who had to cross the Rocky Mountains on the great California route. He spoke at length of their perils to the suffering passenger, who felt none the warmer, and at last gave a groan of weariness.

"How fur did you say 't was now?"

"I do' know's I said, Mis' Tobin," answered the driver, with a frosty laugh. "You see them big pines, and the side of a barn just this way, with them yellow circus bills? That's my three-mile mark."

"Be we got four more to make? Oh, my laws!" mourned Mrs. Tobin. "Urge the beast, can't ye, Jeff 'son? I ain't used to bein' out in such bleak weather. Seems if I couldn't git my breath. I'm all pinched up and wigglin' with shivers now. 'T ain't no use lettin' the hoss go step-a-ty-step, this fashion."

"Landy me!" exclaimed the affronted driver. "I don't see why folks expects me to race with the cars. Everybody that gits in wants me to run the hoss to death on the road. I make a good everage o' time, and that's all I *can* do. Ef you was to go back an' forth every day but Sabbath fur eighteen years, *you'd* want to ease it all you could, and let those thrash the spokes out o' their wheels that wanted to. North Kilby, Mondays, Wednesdays, and Fridays; Sanscrit Pond, Tuesdays, Thu'sdays, an' Saturdays. Me an' the beast's done it eighteen years together, and the creatur' warn't, so to say, young when we begun it, nor I neither. I re'lly didn't know's she'd hold out till this time. There, git up, will ye, old mar'!" as the beast of burden stopped short in the road.

There was a story that Jefferson gave this faithful creature a rest three times a mile, and took four hours for the journey by himself, and longer whenever he had a passenger. But in pleasant weather the road was delightful, and full of people who drove their own conveyances, and liked to stop and talk. There were not many farms, and the third growth of white pines made a pleasant shade, though Jefferson liked to say that when he began to carry the mail his way lay through an open country of stumps and sparse underbrush, where the white pines nowadays completely arched the road.

They had passed the barn with circus posters, and felt colder than ever when they caught sight of the weather-beaten acrobats in their tights.

"My gorry!" exclaimed Widow Tobin, "them pore creatur's looks as cheerless as little birch-trees in snow-time. I hope they dresses 'em warmer this time o' year. Now, there! look at that one jumpin' through the little hoop, will ye?"

"He couldn't git himself through there with two pair o' pants on," answered Mr. Briley. "I expect they must have to keep limber as eels. I used to think, when I was a boy, that 't was the only thing I could ever be reconciled to do for a livin'. I set out to run away an' follow a rovin' showman once, but mother needed me to home. There warn't nobody but me an' the little gals."

"You ain't the only one that's be'n disapp'inted o' their heart's desire," said Mrs. Tobin sadly. "'T warn't so that I could be spared from home to learn the dressmaker's trade."

"'T would a come handy later on, I declare," answered the sympathetic

SARAH ORNE JEWETT

driver, "bein' 's you went an' had such a passel o' gals to clothe an' feed. There, them that's livin' is all well off now, but it must ha' been some inconvenient for ye when they was small."

"Yes, Mr. Briley, but then I've had my mercies, too," said the widow somewhat grudgingly. "I take it master hard now, though, havin' to give up my own home and live round from place to place, if they be my own child'en. There was Ad'line and Susan Ellen fussin' an' bickerin' yesterday about who'd got to have me next; and, Lord be thanked, they both wanted me right off but I hated to hear 'em talkin' of it over. I'd rather live to home, and do for myself."

"I've got consider'ble used to boardin'," said Jefferson, "sence ma'am died, but it made me ache 'long at the fust on't, I tell ye. Bein' on the road's I be, I couldn't do no ways at keepin' house. I should want to keep right there and see to things."

"Course you would," replied Mrs. Tobin, with a sudden inspiration of opportunity which sent a welcome glow all over her. "Course you would, Jeff'son,"—she leaned toward the front seat; "that is to say, onless you had jest the right one to do it for ye."

And Jefferson felt a strange glow also, and a sense of unexpected interest and enjoyment.

"See here, Sister Tobin," he exclaimed with enthusiasm. "Why can't ye take the trouble to shift seats, and come front here long o' me? We could put one buff'lo top o' the other,—they're both wearin' thin,—and set close, and I do' know but we sh'd be more protected ag'inst the weather."

"Well, I couldn't be no colder if I was froze to death," answered the widow, with an amiable simper. "Don't ye let me delay you, nor put you out, Mr. Briley. I don't know's I'd set forth to-day if I'd known't was so cold; but I had all my bundles done up, and I ain't one that puts my hand to the plough an' looks back, 'cordin' to Scriptur'."

"You wouldn't wanted me to ride all them seven miles alone?" asked the gallant Briley sentimentally, as he lifted her down, and helped her up again to the front seat. She was a few years older than he, but they had been schoolmates, and Mrs. Tobin's youthful freshness was suddenly revived to his mind's eye. She had a little farm; there was nobody left at home now but herself, and so she had broken up housekeeping for the winter. Jefferson himself had savings of no mean amount.

They tucked themselves in, and felt better for the change, but there was a sudden awkwardness between them; they had not had time to prepare for an unexpected crisis.

"They say Elder Bickers, over to East Sanscrit, 's been and got married again to a gal that's four year younger than his oldest daughter," proclaimed Mrs. Tobin presently. "Seems to me 't was fool's business."

"I view it so," said the stage-driver. "There's goin' to be a mild open winter for that fam'ly."

"What a joker you be for a man that's had so much responsibility!" smiled Mrs. Tobin, after they had done laughing. "Ain't you never 'fraid, carryin' mail matter and such valuable stuff, that you'll be set on an' robbed, 'specially by night?"

Jefferson braced his feet against the dasher under the worn buffalo skin. "It is kind o' scary, or would be for some folks, but I'd like to see anybody get the better o' me. I go armed, and I don't care who knows it. Some o' them drover men that comes from Canady looks as if they didn't care what they did, but I look 'em right in the eye every time."

"Men folks is brave by natur'," said the widow admiringly. "You know how Tobin would let his fist right out at anybody that ondertook to sass him. Town-meetin' days, if he got disappointed about the way things went, he'd lay 'em out in win'rows; and ef he hadn't been a church-member he'd been a real fightin' character. I was always 'fraid to have him roused, for all he was so willin' and meechin' to home, and set round clever as anybody. My Susan Ellen used to boss him same's the kitten, when she was four year old."

"I've got a kind of a sideways cant to my nose, that Tobin give me when we was to school. I don't know's you ever noticed it," said Mr. Briley. "We was scufflin', as lads will. I never bore him no kind of a grudge. I pitied ye, when he was taken away. I re'lly did, now, Fanny. I liked Tobin first-rate, and I liked you. I used to say you was the han'somest girl to school."

"Lemme see your nose. 'T is all straight, for what I know," said the widow gently, as with a trace of coyness she gave a hasty glance. "I don't know but what 't is warped a little, but nothin' to speak of. You've got real nice features, like your marm's folks."

It was becoming a sentimental occasion, and Jefferson Briley felt that he was in for something more than he had bargained. He hurried the faltering sorrel horse, and began to talk of the weather. It certainly did look like snow, and he was tired of bumping over the frozen road.

"I shouldn't wonder if I hired a hand here another year, and went off out West myself to see the country."

"Why, how you talk!" answered the widow.

"Yes 'm," pursued Jefferson. "'T is tamer here than I like, and I was tellin' 'em yesterday I've got to know this road most too well. I'd like to go out an' ride in the mountains with some o' them great clipper coaches, where the driver don't know one minute but he'll be shot dead the next. They carry an awful sight o' gold down from the mines, I expect."

"I should be scairt to death," said Mrs. Tobin. "What creatur's men folks be to like such things! Well, I do declare."

"Yes," explained the mild little man. "There's sights of desp'radoes makes a han'some livin' out o' followin' them coaches, an' stoppin' an' robbin' 'em clean to the bone. Your money *or* your life!" and he flourished his stub of a whip over the sorrel mare.

"Landy me! you make me run all of a cold creep. Do tell somethin' heartenin', this cold day. I shall dream bad dreams all night."

"They put on black crape over their heads," said the driver mysteriously. "Nobody knows who most on 'em be, and like as not some o' them fellows come o' good families. They've got so they stop the cars, and go right through 'em bold as brass. I could make your hair stand on end, Mis' Tobin,—I could *so!*"

"I hope none on 'em 'll git round our way, I'm sure," said Fanny Tobin. "I don't want to see none on 'em in their crape bunnits comin' after me."

"I ain't goin' to let nobody touch a hair o' your head," and Mr. Briley moved a little nearer, and tucked in the buffaloes again.

"I feel considerable warm to what I did," observed the widow by way of reward.

"There, I used to have my fears," Mr. Briley resumed, with an inward feeling that he never would get to North Kilby depot a single man. "But you see I hadn't nobody but myself to think of. I've got cousins, as you know, but nothin' nearer, and what I've laid up would soon be parted out; and—well, I suppose some folks would think o' me if anything was to happen."

Mrs. Tobin was holding her cloud over her face,—the wind was sharp on that bit of open road,—but she gave an encouraging sound, between a groan and a chirp.

"'T wouldn't be like nothin' to me not to see you drivin' by," she said, after a minute. "I shouldn't know the days o' the week. I says to Susan Ellen last week I was sure 't was Friday, and she said no, 't was Thursday; but next minute you druv by and headin' toward North Kilby, so we found I was right."

"I've got to be a featur' of the landscape," said Mr. Briley plaintively. "This kind o' weather the old mare and me, we wish we was done with it, and could settle down kind o' comfortable. I've been lookin' this good while, as I drove the road, and I've picked me out a piece o' land two or three times. But I can't abide the thought o' buildin',—'t would plague me to death; and both Sister Peak to North Kilby and Mis' Deacon Ash to the Pond, they vie with one another to do well by me, fear I'll like the other stoppin'-place best."

"*I* shouldn't covet livin' long o' neither one o' them women," responded the passenger with some spirit. "I see some o' Mis' Peak's cookin' to a farmers' supper once, when I was visitin' Susan Ellen's folks, an' I says 'Deliver me from sech pale-complected baked beans as them!' and she give a kind of a quack. She was settin' jest at my left hand, and couldn't help hearin' of me. I wouldn't have spoken if I had known, but she needn't have let on they was hers an' make everything unpleasant. 'I guess them beans taste just as well as other folks',' says she, and she wouldn't never speak to me afterward."

"Do' know's I blame her," ventured Mr. Briley. "Women folks is dreadful pudjicky about their cookin'. I've always heard you was one o' the best o' cooks, Mis' Tobin. I know them doughnuts an' things you've give me in times past, when I was drivin' by. Wish I had some on 'em now. I never let on, but Mis' Ash's cookin' 's the best by a long chalk. Mis' Peak's handy about some things, and looks after mendin' of me up."

"It doos seem as if a man o' your years and your quiet make ought to have a home you could call your own," suggested the passenger. "I kind of hate to think o' your bangein' here and boardin' there, and one old woman mendin', and the other settin' ye down to meals that like's not don't agree with ye."

"Lor', now, Mis' Tobin, le's not fuss round no longer," said Mr. Briley impatiently. "You know you covet me same 's I do you."

"I don't nuther. Don't you go an' say fo'lish things you can't stand to."

"I've been tryin' to git a chance to put in a word with you ever sence— Well, I expected you'd want to get your feelin's kind o' calloused after losin' Tobin."

"There's nobody can fill his place," said the widow.

"I do' know but I can fight for ye town-meetin' days, on a pinch," urged Jefferson boldly.

"I never see the beat o' you men fur conceit," and Mrs. Tobin laughed. "I ain't goin' to bother with ye, gone half the time as you be, an' carryin' on with your Mis' Peaks and Mis' Ashes. I dare say you've promised yourself to both on 'em twenty times."

"I hope to gracious if I ever breathed a word to none on 'em!" protested the lover. "'T ain't for lack o' opportunities set afore me, nuther;" and then Mr. Briley craftily kept silence, as if he had made a fair proposal, and expected a definite reply.

The lady of his choice was, as she might have expressed it, much beat about. As she soberly thought, she was getting along in years, and must put up with Jefferson all the rest of the time. It was not likely she would ever have the chance of choosing again, though she was one who liked variety.

Jefferson wasn't much to look at, but he was pleasant and appeared boyish and young-feeling. "I do' know's I should do better," she said unconsciously and half aloud. "Well, yes, Jefferson, sccin' it's you. But we're both on us kind of old to change our situation." Fanny Tobin gave a gentle sigh.

"Hooray!" said Jefferson. "I was scairt you meant to keep me sufferin' here a half an hour. I declare, I'm more pleased than I calc'lated on. An' I expected till lately to die a single man!"

"'T would re'lly have been a shame; 't ain't natur'," said Mrs. Tobin, with confidence. "I don't see how you held out so long with bein' solitary."

"I'll hire a hand to drive for me, and we'll have a good comfortable winter, me an' you an' the old sorrel. I've been promisin' of her a rest this good while."

"Better keep her a steppin'," urged thrifty Mrs. Fanny. "She'll stiffen up master, an' disapp'int ye, come spring."

"You'll have me, now, won't ye, sartin?" pleaded Jefferson, to make sure. "You ain't one o' them that plays with a man's feelin's. Say right out you'll have me."

"I s'pose I shall have to," said Mrs. Tobin somewhat mournfully. "I feel for Mis' Peak an' Mis' Ash, pore creatur's. I expect they'll be hardshipped. They've always been hard-worked, an' may have kind o' looked forward to a little ease. But one on 'em would be left lamentin', anyhow," and she gave a girlish laugh. An air of victory animated the frame of Mrs. Tobin. She felt but twenty-five years of age. In that moment she made plans for cutting her Briley's hair, and making him look smartened-up and ambitious. Then she wished that she knew for certain how much money he had in the bank; not that it would make any difference now. "He needn't bluster none before me," she thought gayly. "He's harmless as a fly."

"Who'd have thought we'd done such a piece of engineerin', when we started out?" inquired the dear one of Mr. Briley's heart, as he tenderly helped her to alight at Susan Ellen's door.

"Both on us, jest the least grain," answered the lover. "Gimme a good smack, now, you clever creatur';" and so they parted. Mr. Briley had been taken on the road in spite of his pistol.

THE MISTRESS OF SYDENHAM PLANTATION

A high wind was blowing from the water into the Beaufort streets,—a wind with as much reckless hilarity as March could give to her breezes, but soft and spring-like, almost early-summer-like, in its warmth.

In the gardens of the old Southern houses that stood along the bay, roses and petisporum-trees were blooming, with their delicious fragrance. It was the time of wistarias and wild white lilies, of the last yellow jas-mines and the first Cherokee roses. It was the Saturday before Easter Sunday.

In the quaint churchyard of old St. Helena's Church, a little way from the bay, young figures were busy among the graves with industrious gardening. At first sight, one might have thought that this pretty service was rendered only from loving sentiments of loyalty to one's ancestors, for under the great live-oaks, the sturdy brick walls about the family burying-places and the gravestones themselves were moss-grown and ancient-looking; yet here and there the wounded look of the earth appealed to the eye, and betrayed a new-made grave. The old sarcophagi and heavy tablets of the historic Beaufort families stood side by side with plain wooden crosses. The armorial bearings and long epitaphs of the one and the brief lettering of the other suggested the changes that had come with the war to these families, yet somehow the wooden cross touched one's heart with closer sympathy. The padlocked gates to the small inclosures stood open, while gentle girls passed in and out with their Easter flowers of remembrance. On the high churchyard wall and great gate-posts perched many a mocking-bird, and the golden light changed the twilight under the live-oaks to a misty warmth of color. The birds began to sing louder; the gray moss that hung from the heavy boughs swayed less and less, and gave the place a look of pensive silence.

In the church itself, most of the palms and rose branches were already in place for the next day's feast, and the old organ followed a fresh young voice that was being trained for the Easter anthem. The five doors of the church were standing open. On the steps of that eastern door which opened midway up the side aisle, where the morning sun had shone in upon the white faces of a hospital in war-time,—in this eastern doorway sat two young women.

"I was just thinking," one was saying to the other, "that for the first time Mistress Sydenham has forgotten to keep this day. You know that when she has forgotten everything and everybody else, she has known when Easter came, and has brought flowers to her graves."

"Has she been more feeble lately, do you think?" asked the younger of the two. "Mamma saw her the other day, and thought that she seemed more like herself; but she looked very old, too. She told mamma to bring her dolls, and she would give her some bits of silk to make them gowns. Poor mamma! and she had just been wondering how she could manage to get us ready for summer, this year,—Célestine and me," and the speaker smiled wistfully.

"It is a mercy that the dear old lady did forget all that happened;" and the friends brushed some last bits of leaves from their skirts, and rose and walked away together through the churchyard.

The ancient church waited through another Easter Even, with its flowers and long memory of prayer and praise. The great earthquake had touched it lightly, time had colored it softly, and the earthly bodies of its children were gathered near its walls in peaceful sleep.

From one of the high houses which stood fronting the sea, with their airy balconies and colonnades, had come a small, slender figure, like some shy, dark thing of twilight out into the bright sunshine. The street was empty, for the most part; before one or two of the cheap German shops a group of men watched the little old lady step proudly by. She was a very stately gentlewoman, for one so small and thin; she was feeble, too, and bending somewhat with the weight of years, but there was true elegance and dignity in the way she moved, and those who saw her—persons who shuffled when they walked, and boasted loudly of the fallen pride of the South—were struck with sudden deference and admiration. Behind the lady walked a gray-headed negro, a man who was troubled in spirit, who sometimes gained a step or two, and offered an anxious but quite unheeded remonstrance. He was a poor, tottering old fellow; he wore a threadbare evening coat that might have belonged to his late master thirty years before.

The pair went slowly along the bay street to the end of a row of new shops, and the lady turned decidedly toward the water, and approached the ferry-steps. Her servitor groaned aloud, but waited in respectful helplessness. There was a group of negro children on the steps, employed in the dangerous business of crab-fishing; at the foot, in his flat-bottomed boat, sat a wondering negro lad, who looked up in apprehension at his passengers. The lady seemed like a ghost. Old Peter,—with whose scorn of modern beings and their ways he was partially familiar,—old Peter was making frantic signs to him to put out from shore. But the lady's calm desire for obedience prevailed, and presently, out of the knot of idlers that gathered quickly, one, more chivalrous than the rest, helped the strange adventurers down into the boat. It was the fashion to laugh and joke, in Beaufort, when anything unusual was happening before the eyes of the younger part of the colored population; but as the ferryman pushed off from shore, even the crab-fishers kept awe-struck silence, and there were speechless, open mouths and much questioning of eyes that showed their whites in vain. Somehow or other, before the boat was out of hail, long before it had passed the first bank of raccoon oysters, the tide being at the ebb, it was known by fifty people that for the first time in more than twenty years the mistress of the old Sydenham plantation on St. Helena's Island had taken it into her poor daft head to go to look after her estates, her crops, and her people. Everybody knew that her estates had been confiscated during the war; that her people owned it themselves now, in three and five and even twenty acre lots; that her crops of rice and Sea Island cotton were theirs, planted and hoed and harvested on their own account. All these years she had forgotten Sydenham, and the live-oak avenue, and the outlook across the water to the Hunting Islands, where the deer ran wild; she had forgotten the war; she had forgotten her children and her husband, except that they had gone away,—the graves to which she carried Easter flowers were her mother's and her father's graves,—and her life was spent in a strange dream.

Old Peter sat facing her in the boat; the ferryman pulled lustily at his oars, and they moved quickly along in the ebbing tide. The ferryman longed to get his freight safely across; he was in a fret of discomfort whenever he looked at the clear-cut, eager face before him in the stern. How still and straight the old mistress sat! Where was she going? He was awed by her presence, and took refuge, as he rowed, in needless talk about the coming of the sandflies and the great drum-fish to Beaufort waters. But Peter had clasped his hands together and bowed his old back, as if he did not dare to look anywhere but at the bottom of the boat. Peter was still groaning softly; the old lady was looking back over the water to the row of fine houses, the once luxurious summer homes of Rhetts and Barnwells, of many a famous household now scattered and impoverished. The ferryman had heard of more one than bereft lady or gentleman who lived in seclusion in the old houses. He knew that Peter still served a mysterious mistress with exact devotion, while most of the elderly colored men and women who had formed the retinues of the old families were following their own affairs, far and wide.

"Oh, Lord, ole mis'! what kin I go to do?" mumbled Peter, with his head in his hands. "Thar'll be nothin' to see. Po' ole mis', I do' kno' what you say. Trouble, trouble!"

But the mistress of Sydenham plantation had a way of speaking but seldom, and of rarely listening to what any one was pleased to say in return. Out of the mistiness of her clouded brain a thought had come with unwonted clearness. She must go to the island: her husband and sons were detained at a distance; it was the time of year to look after corn and cotton; she must attend to her house and her slaves. The remembrance of that news of battle and of the three deaths that had left her widowed and childless had faded away in the illness it had brought. She never comprehended her loss; she was like one bewitched into indifference; she remembered something of her youth, and kept a simple routine of daily life, and that was all.

"I t'ought she done fo'git ebryt'ing," groaned Peter again. "O Lord, hab mercy on ole mis'!"

The landing-place on Ladies' Island was steep and sandy, and the oarsman watched Peter help the strange passenger up the ascent with a sense of blessed relief. He pushed off a little way into the stream, for better self-defense. At the top of the bluff was a rough shed, built for shelter, and Peter looked about him eagerly, while his mistress stood, expectant and imperious, in the shade of a pride of India tree, that grew among the live-oaks and pines of a wild thicket. He was wretched with a sense of her discomfort, though she gave no sign of it. He had learned to know by instinct all that was unspoken. In the old times she would have found four oarsmen waiting with a cushioned boat at the ferry; she would have found a saddle-horse or a carriage ready for her on Ladies' Island for the five miles' journey, but the carriage had not come. The poor gray-headed old man recognized her displeasure. He was her only slave left, if she did but know it.

"Fo' Gord's sake, git me some kin' of a cart. Ole mis', she done wake up and mean to go out to Syd'n'am dis day," urged Peter. "Who dis hoss an' kyart in de shed? Who make dese track wid huffs jus' now, like dey done ride by? Yo' go git somebody fo' me, or she be right mad, shore."

The elderly guardian of the shed, who was also of the old *régime*, hobbled away quickly, and backed out a steer that was broken to harness, and a rickety two-wheeled cart. Their owner had left them there for some hours, and had crossed the ferry to Beaufort. Old mistress must be obeyed, and they looked toward her beseechingly where she

SARAH ORNE JEWETT

was waiting, deprecating her disapproval of this poor apology for a conveyance. The lady long since had ceased to concern herself with the outward shapes of things; she accepted this possibility of carrying out her plans, and they lifted her light figure to the chair, in the cart's end, while Peter mounted before her with all a coachman's dignity,—he once had his ambitions of being her coachman,—and they moved slowly away through the deep sand.

"My Gord A'mighty, look out fo' us now," said Peter over and over. "Ole mis', she done fo'git, good Lord, she done fo'git how de Good Marsa up dere done took f'om her ebryt'ing; she 'spect now she find Syd'n'am all de same like's it was 'fo' de war. She ain't know 'bout what's been sence day of de gun-shoot on Port Royal and dar-away. O Lord A'mighty, yo' know how yo' stove her po' head wid dem gun-shoot; be easy to ole mis'."

But as Peter pleaded in the love and sorrow of his heart, the lady who sat behind him was unconscious of any cause for grief. Some sweet vagaries in her own mind were matched to the loveliness of the day. All her childhood, spent among the rustic scenes of these fertile Sea Islands, was yielding for her now an undefined pleasantness of association. The straight-stemmed palmettos stood out with picturesque clearness against the great level fields, with their straight furrows running out of sight. Figures of men and women followed the furrow paths slowly; here were men and horses bending to the ploughshare, and there women and children sowed with steady hand the rich seed of their crops. There were touches of color in the head kerchiefs; there were sounds of songs as the people worked,—not gay songs of the evening, but some repeated line of a hymn, to steady the patient feet and make the work go faster,—the unconscious music of the blacks, who sing as the beetle drones or the cricket chirps slowly under the dry grass. It had a look of permanence, this cotton-planting. It was a thing to paint, to relate itself to the permanence of art, an everlasting duty of mankind; terrible if a thing of force, and compulsion and for another's gain, but the birthright of the children of Adam, and not unrewarded nor unnatural when one drew by it one's own life from the earth.

Peter glanced through the hedge-rows furtively, this way and that. What would his mistress say to the cabins that were scattered all about the fields now, and that were no longer put together in the long lines of the quarters? He looked down a deserted lane, where he well remembered fifty cabins on each side of the way. It was gay there of a summer evening; the old times had not been without their pleasures, and the poor old man's heart leaped with the vague delight of his memories. He had never been on the block; he was born and bred at old Sydenham; he had been trusted in house and field.

"I done like dem ole times de best," ventures Peter, presently, to his unresponding companion. "Dere was good 'bout dem times. I say I like de ole times good as any. Young folks may be a change f'om me."

He was growing gray in the face with apprehension; he did not dare to disobey.

The slow-footed beast of burden was carrying them toward Sydenham step by step, and he dreaded the moment of arrival. He was like a mesmerized creature, who can only obey the force of a directing will; but under pretense of handling the steer's harness, he got stiffly to the ground to look at his mistress. He could not turn to face her, as he sat in the cart; he could not drive any longer and feel her there behind him. The silence was too great. It was a relief to see her placid face, and to see even a more youthful look in its worn lines. She had been a very beautiful woman in her young days. And a solemn awe fell upon Peter's tender heart, lest the veil might be lifting from her hidden past, and there, alone with him on the old plantation, she would die of grief and pain. God only knew what might happen! The old man mounted to his seat, and again they plodded on.

"Peter," said the mistress,—he was always frightened when she spoke,—"Peter, we must hurry. I was late in starting. I have a great deal to do. Urge the horses."

"Yas, mis',—yas, mis'," and Peter laughed aloud nervously, and brandished his sassafras switch, while the steer hastened a little. They had come almost to the gates.

"Who are these?" the stately wayfarer asked once, as they met some persons who gazed at them in astonishment.

"I 'spect dem de good ladies f'om de Norf, what come down to show de cullud folks how to do readin'," answered Peter bravely. "It do look kind o' comfo'ble over here," he added wistfully, half to himself. He could not understand even now how oblivious she was of the great changes on St. Helena's.

There were curious eyes watching from the fields, and here by the roadside an aged black woman came to her cabin door.

"Lord!" exclaimed Peter, "what kin I do now? An' ole Sibyl, she's done crazy too, and dey'll be mischievous together."

The steer could not be hurried past, and Sibyl came and leaned against the wheel. "Mornin', mistis," said Sibyl, "an' yo' too, Peter. How's all? Day ob judgment's comin' in mornin'! Some nice buttermilk? I done git rich; t'at's my cow," and she pointed to the field and chuckled. Peter felt as if his brain were turning. "Bless de Lord, I no more slave," said old Sibyl, looking up with impudent scrutiny at her old mistress's impassive face. "Yo' know Mars' Middleton, what yo' buy me f'om? He my foster-brother; we push away from same breast. He got trouble, po' gen'elman; he sorry to sell Sibyl; he give me silver dollar dat day, an' feel bad. 'Neber min', I say. I get good mistis, young mistis at Sydenham. I like her well, I did so. I pick my two hunderd poun' all days, an' I ain't whipped. Too bad sold me, po' Mars' Middleton, but he in trouble. He done come see me last plantin'," Sibyl went on proudly. "Oh, Gord, he grown ole and poor-lookin'. He come in, just in dat do', an' he say, 'Sibyl, I long an' long to see you, an' now I see you;' an' he kiss an' kiss me. An' dere's one wide ribber o' Jordan, an' we'll soon be dere, black an' white. I was right glad I see ole Mars' Middleton 'fore I die."

The old creature poured forth the one story of her great joy and pride; she had told it a thousand times. It had happened, not the last planting, but many plantings ago. It remained clear when everything else was confused. There was no knowing what she might say next. She began to take the strange steps of a slow dance, and Peter urged his steer forward, while his mistress said suddenly, "Good-by, Sibyl. I am glad you are doing so well," with a strange irrelevancy of graciousness. It was in the old days before the war that Sibyl had fallen insensible, one day, in the cotton-field. Did her mistress think that it was still that year, and—Peter's mind could not puzzle out this awful day of anxiety.

They turned at last into the live-oak avenue,—they had only another half mile to go; and here, in the place where the lady had closest association, her memory was suddenly revived almost to clearness. She began to hurry Peter impatiently; it was a mischance that she had not been met at the ferry. She was going to see to putting the house in order, and the women were all waiting. It was autumn, and they were going to move over from Beaufort; it was spring next moment, and she had to talk with her overseers. The old imperiousness flashed out. Did not Peter know that his master was kept at the front, and the young gentlemen were with him, and their regiment was going into action? It was a blessing to come over and forget it all, but Peter must drive, drive. They had taken no care of the avenue; how the trees were broken in the storm! The house needed—They were going to move the next day but one, and nothing was ready. A party of gentlemen were coming from Charleston in the morning!—

They passed the turn of the avenue; they came out to the open lawn, and the steer stopped and began to browse. Peter shook from head to foot. He climbed down by the wheel, and turned his face slowly. "Ole mis'!" he said feebly. "*Ole mis'!*"

She was looking off into space. The cart jerked as it moved after the feeding steer. The mistress of Sydenham plantation had sought her home in vain. The crumbled, fallen chimneys of the house were there among the weeds, and that was all.

ON CHRISTMAS DAY AND EASTER Day, many an old man and woman come into St. Helena's Church who are not seen there the rest of the year. There are not a few recluses in the parish, who come to listen to their teacher and to the familiar prayers, read with touching earnestness and simplicity, as one seldom hears the prayers read anywhere. This Easter morning dawned clear and bright, as Easter morning should. The fresh-bloomed roses and lilies were put in their places. There was no touch of paid hands anywhere, and the fragrance blew softly about the church. As you sat in your pew, you could look out through the wide-opened doors, and see the drooping branches, and the birds as they sat singing on the gravestones. The sad faces of the old people, the cheerful faces of the young, passed by up the aisle. One figure came to sit alone in one of the pews, to bend its head in prayer after the ancient habit. Peter led her, as usual, to the broad-aisle doorway, and helped her, stumbling himself, up the steps, and many eyes filled with tears as his mistress went to her place. Even the tragic moment of yesterday was lost already in the acquiescence of her mind, as the calm sea shines back to the morning sun when another wreck has gone down.

THE TOWN POOR

Mrs. William Trimble and Miss Rebecca Wright were driving along Hampden east road, one afternoon in early spring. Their progress was slow. Mrs. Trimble's sorrel horse was old and stiff, and the wheels were clogged by day mud. The frost was not yet out of the ground, although the snow was nearly gone, except in a few places on the north side of the woods, or where it had drifted all winter against a length of fence.

"There must be a good deal o' snow to the nor'ard of us yet," said weather-wise Mrs. Trimble. "I feel it in the air; 't is more than the ground-damp. We ain't goin' to have real nice weather till the up-country snow's all gone."

"I heard say yesterday that there was good sleddin' yet, all up through Parsley," responded Miss Wright. "I shouldn't like to live in them northern places. My cousin Ellen's husband was a Parsley man, an' he was obliged, as you may have heard, to go up north to his father's second wife's funeral; got back day before yesterday. 'T was about twenty-one miles, an' they started on wheels; but when they'd gone nine or ten miles, they found 't was no sort o' use, an' left their wagon an' took a sleigh. The man that owned it charged 'em four an' six, too. I shouldn't have thought he would; they told him they was goin' to a funeral; an' they had their own buffaloes an' everything."

"Well, I expect it's a good deal harder scratching up that way; they have to git money where they can; the farms is very poor as you go north," suggested Mrs. Trimble kindly. "'T ain't none too rich a country where we be, but I've always been grateful I wa'n't born up to Parsley."

The old horse plodded along, and the sun, coming out from the heavy spring clouds, sent a sudden shine of light along the muddy road. Sister Wright drew her large veil forward over the high brim of her bonnet. She was not used to driving, or to being much in the open air; but Mrs. Trimble was an active business woman, and looked after her own affairs herself, in all weathers. The late Mr. Trimble had left her a good farm, but not much ready money, and it was often said that she was better off in the end than if he had lived. She regretted his loss deeply, however; it was impossible for her to speak of him, even to intimate friends, without emotion, and nobody had ever hinted that this emotion was insincere. She was most warm-hearted and generous, and in her limited way played the part of Lady Bountiful in the town of Hampden.

"Why, there's where the Bray girls lives, ain't it?" she exclaimed, as, beyond a thicket of witch-hazel and scrub-oak, they came in sight of a weather-beaten, solitary farmhouse. The barn was too far away for thrift or comfort, and they could see long lines of light between the shrunken boards as they came nearer. The fields looked both stony and sodden. Somehow, even Parsley itself could be hardly more forlorn.

"Yes'm," said Miss Wright, "that's where they live now, poor things. I know the place, though I ain't been up here for years. You don't suppose, Mis' Trimble—I ain't seen the girls out to meetin' all winter. I've re'lly been covetin'"—

"Why, yes, Rebecca, of course we could stop," answered Mrs. Trimble heartily. "The exercises was over earlier 'n I expected, an' you're goin' to remain over night long o' me, you know. There won't be no tea till we git there, so we can't be late. I'm in the habit o' sendin' a basket to the Bray girls when any o' our folks is comin' this way, but I ain't been to see 'em since they moved up here. Why, it must be a good deal over a year ago. I know 't was in the late winter they had to make the move. 'T was cruel hard, I must say, an' if I hadn't been down with my pleurisy fever I'd have stirred round an' done somethin' about it. There was a good deal o' sickness at the time, an'—well, 't was kind o' rushed through, breakin' of 'em up, an' lots o' folks blamed the selec'men; but when 't was done, 't was done, an' nobody took holt to undo it. Ann an' Mandy looked same's ever when they come to meetin', 'long in the summer,—kind o' wishful, perhaps. They've always sent me word they was gittin' on pretty comfortable."

"That would be their way," said Rebecca Wright. "They never was any hand to complain, though Mandy's less cheerful than Ann. If Mandy'd been spared such poor eyesight, an' Ann hadn't got her lame wrist that wa'n't set right, they'd kep' off the town fast enough. They both shed tears when they talked to me about havin' to break up, when I went to see 'em before I went over to brother Asa's. You see we was brought up neighbors, an' we went to school together, the Brays an' me. 'T was a special Providence brought us home this road, I've been so covetin' a chance to git to see 'em. My lameness hampers me."

"I'm glad we come this way, myself," said Mrs. Trimble.

"I'd like to see just how they fare," Miss Rebecca Wright continued. "They give their consent to goin' on the town because they knew they'd got to be dependent, an' so they felt 't would come easier for all than for a few to help 'em. They acted real dignified an' right-minded, contrary to what most do in such cases, but they was dreadful anxious to see who would bid 'em off, town-meeting day; they did so hope 't would be somebody right in the village. I just sat down an' cried good when I found Abel Janes's folks had got hold of 'em. They always had the name of bein' slack an' poor-spirited, an' they did it just for what they got out o' the town. The selectmen this last year ain't what we have had. I hope they've been considerate about the Bray girls."

"I should have be'n more considerate about fetchin' of you over," apologized Mrs. Trimble. "I've got my horse, an' you 're lame-footed; 't is too far for you to come. But time does slip away with busy folks, an' I forgit a good deal I ought to remember."

"There's nobody more considerate than you be," protested Miss Rebecca Wright.

Mrs. Trimble made no answer, but took out her whip and gently touched the sorrel horse, who walked considerably faster, but did not think it worth while to trot. It was a long, round-about way to the house, farther down the road and up a lane.

"I never had any opinion of the Bray girls' father, leavin' 'em as he did," said Mrs. Trimble.

"He was much praised in his time, though there was always some said his early life hadn't been up to the mark," explained her companion. "He was a great favorite of our then preacher, the Reverend Daniel Longbrother. They did a good deal for the parish, but they did it their own way. Deacon Bray was one that did his part in the repairs without urging. You know 't was in his time the first repairs was made, when they got out the old soundin'-board an' them handsome square pews. It cost an awful sight o' money, too. They hadn't done payin' up that debt when they set to alter it again an' git the walls frescoed. My grandmother was one that always spoke her mind right out, an' she was dreadful opposed to breakin' up the square pews where she'd always set. They was countin' up what 't would cost in parish meetin', an' she riz right up an' said 't wouldn't cost nothin' to let 'em stay, an' there wa'n't a house carpenter left in the parish that could do such nice work, an' time would come when the great-grandchildren would give their eye-teeth to have the old meetin'-house look just as it did then. But haul the inside to pieces they would and did."

"There come to be a real fight over it, didn't there?" agreed Mrs. Trimble soothingly. "Well, 't wa'n't good taste. I remember the old house well. I come here as a child to visit a cousin o' mother's, an' Mr. Trimble's folks was neighbors, an' we was drawed to each other then, young's we was. Mr. Trimble spoke of it many's the time,—that first time he ever see me, in a leghorn hat with a feather; 't was one that mother had, an' pressed over."

"When I think of them old sermons that used to be preached in that old meetin'-house of all, I'm glad it's altered over, so's not to remind folks," said Miss Rebecca Wright, after a suitable pause. "Them old brimstone discourses, you know, Mis' Trimble. Preachers is far more reasonable, nowadays. Why, I set an' thought, last Sabbath, as I listened, that if old Mr. Longbrother an' Deacon Bray could hear the difference they 'd crack the ground over 'em like pole beans, an' come right up 'long side their headstones."

Mrs. Trimble laughed heartily, and shook the reins three or four times by way of emphasis. "There's no gitting round you," she said, much pleased. "I should think Deacon Bray would want to rise, any way, if 't was so he could, an' knew how his poor girls was farin'. A man ought to provide for his folks he's got to leave behind him, specially if they're women. To be sure, they had their little home; but we've seen how, with all their industrious ways, they hadn't means to keep it. I s'pose he thought he'd got time enough to lay by, when he give so generous in collections; but he didn't lay by, an' there they be. He might have took lessons from the squirrels: even them little wild creator's makes them their winter hoards, an' men-folks ought to know enough if squirrels does. 'Be just before you are generous:' that's what was always set for the B's in the copy-books, when I was to school, and it often runs through my mind."

"'As for man, his days are as grass,'—that was for A; the two go well together," added Miss Rebecca Wright soberly. "My good gracious, ain't this a starved-lookin' place? It makes me ache to think them nice Bray girls has to brook it here."

The sorrel horse, though somewhat puzzled by an unexpected deviation from his homeward way, willingly came to a stand by the gnawed corner of the door-yard fence, which evidently served as hitching-place. Two or three ragged old hens were picking about the yard, and at last a face appeared at the kitchen window, tied up in a handkerchief, as if it were a case of toothache. By the time our friends reached the side door next this window, Mrs. Janes came disconsolately to open it for them, shutting it again as soon as possible, though the air felt more chilly inside the house.

"Take seats," said Mrs. Janes briefly. "You'll have to see me just as I be. I have been suffering these four days with the ague, and everything to do. Mr. Janes is to court, on the jury. 'T was inconvenient to spare him. I should be pleased to have you lay off your things."

Comfortable Mrs. Trimble looked about the cheerless kitchen, and could not think of anything to say; so she smiled blandly and shook her head in answer to the invitation. "We'll just set a few minutes with you, to pass the time o' day, an' then we must go in an' have a word with the Miss Brays, bein' old acquaintance. It ain't been so we could git to call on 'em before. I don't know's you're acquainted with Miss R'becca Wright. She's been out of town a good deal."

"I heard she was stopping over to Plainfields with her brother's folks," replied Mrs. Janes, rocking herself with irregular motion, as she sat close to the stove. "Got back some time in the fall, I believe?"

"Yes'm," said Miss Rebecca, with an undue sense of guilt and conviction. "We've been to the installation over to the East Parish, an' thought we'd stop in; we took this road home to see if 't was any better. How is the Miss Brays gettin' on?"

"They're well's common," answered Mrs. Janes grudgingly. "I was put out with Mr. Janes for fetchin' of 'em here, with all I've got to do, an' I own I was kind o' surly to 'em 'long to the first of it. He gits the money from the town, an' it helps him out; but he bid 'em off for five dollars a month, an' we can't do much for 'em at no such price as that. I went an' dealt with the selec'men, an' made 'em promise to find their firewood an' some other things extra. They was glad to get rid o' the matter the fourth time I went, an' would ha' promised 'most anything. But Mr. Janes don't keep me half the time in oven-wood, he's off so much, an' we was cramped o' room, any way. I have to store things up garrit a good deal, an' that keeps me trampin' right through their room. I do the best for 'em I can, Mis' Trimble, but 't ain't so easy for me as 't is for you, with all your means to do with."

The poor woman looked pinched and miserable herself, though it was evident that she had no gift at house or home keeping. Mrs. Trimble's heart was wrung with pain, as she thought of the unwelcome inmates of such a place; but she held her peace bravely, while Miss Rebecca again gave some brief information in regard to the installation.

"You go right up them back stairs," the hostess directed at last. "I'm glad some o' you church folks has seen fit to come an' visit 'em. There ain't been nobody here this long spell, an' they've aged a sight since they come. They always send down a taste out of your baskets, Mis' Trimble, an' I relish it, I tell you. I'll shut the door after you, if you don't object. I feel every draught o' cold air."

"I've always heard she was a great hand to make a poor mouth. Wa'n't she from somewheres up Parsley way?" whispered Miss Rebecca, as they stumbled in the half-light.

"Poor meechin' body, wherever she come from," replied Mrs. Trimble, as she knocked at the door.

There was silence for a moment after this unusual sound; then one of the Bray sisters opened the door. The eager guests stared into a small, low room, brown with age, and gray, too, as if former dust and cobwebs could not be made wholly to disappear. The two elderly women who stood there looked like captives. Their withered faces wore a look of apprehension, and the room itself was more bare and plain than was fitting to their evident refinement of character and self-respect. There was an uncovered small table in the middle of the floor, with some crackers on a plate; and, for some reason or other, this added a great deal to the general desolation.

But Miss Ann Bray, the elder sister, who carried her right arm in a sling, with piteously drooping fingers, gazed at the visitors with radiant joy. She had not seen them arrive.

The one window gave only the view at the back of the house, across the fields, and their coming was indeed a surprise. The next minute she was laughing and crying together. "Oh, sister!" she said, "if here ain't our dear Mis' Trimble!—an' my heart o' goodness, 't is 'Becca Wright, too! What dear good creatur's you be! I've felt all day as if something good was goin' to happen, an' was just sayin' to myself 't was most sundown now, but I wouldn't let on to Mandany I'd give up hope quite yet. You see, the scissors stuck in the floor this very mornin' an' it's always a reliable sign. There, I've got to kiss ye both again!"

"I don't know where we can all set," lamented sister Mandana. "There ain't but the one chair an' the bed; t' other chair's too rickety; an' we've been promised another these ten days; but first they've forgot it, an' next Mis' Janes can't spare it,—one excuse an' another. I am goin' to git a stump o' wood an' nail a board on to it, when I can git outdoor again," said Mandana, in a plaintive voice. "There, I ain't goin' to complain o' nothin', now you've come," she added; and the guests sat down, Mrs. Trimble, as was proper, in the one chair.

"We've sat on the bed many's the time with you, 'Beeca, an' talked over our girl nonsense, ain't we? You know where 't was—in the little back bedroom we had when we was girls, an' used to peek out at our beaux through the strings o' mornin'-glories," laughed Ann Bray delightedly, her thin face shining more and more with joy. "I brought some o' them mornin'-glory seeds along when we come away, we'd raised 'em so many years; an' we got 'em started all right, but the hens found 'em out. I declare I chased them poor hens, foolish as 't was; but the mornin'-glories I'd counted on a sight to remind me o' home. You see, our debts was so large, after my long sickness an' all, that we didn't feel 't was right to keep back anything we could help from the auction."

It was impossible for any one to speak for a moment or two; the sisters felt their own uprooted condition afresh, and their guests for the first time really comprehended the piteous contrast between that neat little village house, which now seemed a palace of comfort, and this cold, unpainted upper room in the remote Janes farmhouse. It was an unwelcome thought to Mrs. Trimble that the well-to-do town of Hampden could provide no better for its poor than this, and her round face flushed with resentment and the shame of personal responsibility. "The girls shall be well settled in the village before another winter, if I pay their board myself," she made an inward resolution, and took another almost tearful look at the broken stove, the miserable bed, and the sisters' one hair-covered trunk, on which Mandana was sitting. But the poor place was filled with a golden spirit of hospitality.

Rebecca was again discoursing eloquently of the installation; it was so much easier to speak of general subjects, and the sisters had evidently been longing to hear some news. Since the late summer they had not been to church, and presently Mrs. Trimble asked the reason.

"Now, don't you go to pouring out our woes, Mandy!" begged little old Ann, looking shy and almost girlish, and as if she insisted upon playing that life was still all before them and all pleasure. "Don't you go to spoilin' their visit with our complaints! They know well's we do that changes must come, an' we'd been so wonted to our home things that this come hard at first; but then they felt for us, I know just as well's can be. 'T will soon be summer again, an' 't is real pleasant right out in the fields here, when there ain't too hot a spell. I've got to know a sight o' singin' birds since we come."

"Give me the folks I've always known," sighed the younger sister, who looked older than Miss Ann, and less even-tempered. "You may have your birds, if you want 'em. I do re'lly long to go to meetin' an' see folks go by up the aisle. Now, I will speak of it, Ann, whatever you say. We need, each of us, a pair o' good stout shoes an' rubbers,—ours are all wore out; an' we've asked an' asked, an' they never think to bring 'em, an'"—

Poor old Mandana, on the trunk, covered her face with her arms and sobbed aloud. The elder sister stood over her, and patted her on the thin shoulder like a child, and tried to comfort her. It crossed Mrs. Trimble's mind that it was not the first time one had wept and the other had comforted. The sad scene must have been repeated many times in that long, drear winter. She would see them forever after in her mind as fixed as a picture, and her own tears fell fast.

"You didn't see Mis' Janes's cunning little boy, the next one to the baby, did you?" asked Ann Bray, turning round quickly at last, and going cheerfully on with the conversation. "Now, hush, Mandy, dear; they'll think you're childish! He's a dear, friendly little creatur', an' likes to stay with us a good deal, though we feel's if it 't was too cold for him, now we are waitin' to get us more wood."

"When I think of the acres o' woodland in this town!" groaned Rebecca Wright. "I believe I'm goin' to preach next Sunday, 'stead o' the minister, an' I'll make the sparks fly. I've always heard the saying, 'What's everybody's business is nobody's business,' an' I've come to believe it."

"Now, don't you, 'Becca. You've happened on a kind of a poor time with us, but we've got more belongings than you see here, an' a good large cluset, where we can store those things there ain't room to have about. You an' Miss Trimble have happened on a kind of poor day, you know. Soon's I git me some stout shoes an' rubbers, as Mandy says, I can fetch home plenty o' little dry boughs o' pine; you remember I was always a great hand to roam in the woods? If we could only have a front room, so 't we could look out on the road an' see passin', an' was shod for meetin', I don' know's we should complain. Now we're just goin' to give you what we've got, an' make out with a good welcome. We make more tea 'n we want in the mornin', an' then let the fire go down, since 't has been so mild. We've got a *good* cluset" (disappearing as she spoke), "an' I know this to be good tea, 'cause it's some o' yourn, Mis' Trimble. An' here's our sprigged chiny cups that R'becca knows by sight, if Mis' Trimble don't. We kep' out four of 'em, an' put the even half dozen with the rest of the auction stuff. I've often wondered who 'd got 'em, but I never asked, for fear 't would be somebody that would distress us. They was mother's, you know."

The four cups were poured, and the little table pushed to the bed, where Rebecca Wright still sat, and Mandana, wiping her eyes, came

SARAH ORNE JEWETT

and joined her. Mrs. Trimble sat in her chair at the end, and Ann trotted about the room in pleased content for a while, and in and out of the closet, as if she still had much to do; then she came and stood opposite Mrs. Trimble. She was very short and small, and there was no painful sense of her being obliged to stand. The four cups were not quite full of cold tea, but there was a clean old tablecloth folded double, and a plate with three pairs of crackers neatly piled, and a small—it must be owned, a very small—piece of hard white cheese. Then, for a treat, in a glass dish, there was a little preserved peach, the last—Miss Rebecca knew it instinctively—of the household stores brought from their old home. It was very sugary, this bit of peach; and as she helped her guests and sister Mandy, Miss Ann Bray said, half unconsciously, as she often had said with less reason in the old days, "Our preserves ain't so good as usual this year; this is beginning to candy." Both the guests protested, while Rebecca added that the taste of it carried her back, and made her feel young again. The Brays had always managed to keep one or two peach-trees alive in their corner of a garden. "I've been keeping this preserve for a treat," said her friend. "I'm glad to have you eat some, 'Becca. Last summer I often wished you was home an' could come an' see us, 'stead o' being away off to Plainfields."

The crackers did not taste too dry. Miss Ann took the last of the peach on her own cracker; there could not have been quite a small spoonful, after the others were helped, but she asked them first if they would not have some more. Then there was a silence, and in the silence a wave of tender feeling rose high in the hearts of the four elderly women. At this moment the setting sun flooded the poor plain room with light; the unpainted wood was all of a golden-brown, and Ann Bray, with her gray hair and aged face, stood at the head of the table in a kind of aureole. Mrs. Trimble's face was all aquiver as she looked at her; she thought of the text about two or three being gathered together, and was half afraid.

"I believe we ought to 've asked Mis' Janes if she wouldn't come up," said Ann. "She's real good feelin', but she's had it very hard, an' gits discouraged. I can't find that she's ever had anything real pleasant to look back to, as we have. There, next time we'll make a good heartenin' time for her too."

THE SORREL HORSE HAD TAKEN a long nap by the gnawed fence-rail, and the cool air after sundown made him impatient to be gone. The two friends jolted homeward in the gathering darkness, through the stiffening mud, and neither Mrs. Trimble nor Rebecca Wright said a word until they were out of sight as well as out of sound of the Janes house. Time must elapse before they could reach a more familiar part of the road and resume conversation on its natural level.

"I consider myself to blame," insisted Mrs. Trimble at last. "I haven't no words of accusation for nobody else, an' I ain't one to take comfort in calling names to the board o' selec'*men*. I make no reproaches, an' I take it all on my own shoulders; but I'm goin' to stir about me, I tell you! I shall begin early to-morrow. They're goin' back to their own house,—it's been stand-in' empty all winter,—an' the town's goin' to give 'em the rent an' what firewood they need; it won't come to more than the board's payin' out now. An' you an' me'll take this same horse an' wagon, an' ride an' go afoot by turns, an' git means enough together to buy back their furniture an' whatever was sold at that plaguey auction; an' then we'll put it all back, an' tell 'em they've got to move to a new place, an' just carry 'em right back again where they come from. An' don't you never tell, R'becca, but here I be a widow woman, layin' up what I make from my farm for nobody knows who, an' I'm goin' to do for them Bray girls all I'm a mind to. I should be sca't to wake up in heaven, an' hear anybody there ask how the Bray girls was. Don't talk to me about the town o' Hampden, an' don't ever let me hear the name o' town poor! I'm ashamed to go home an' see what's set out for supper. I wish I'd brought 'em right along."

"I was goin' to ask if we couldn't git the new doctor to go up an' do somethin' for poor Ann's arm," said Miss Rebecca. "They say he's very smart. If she could get so's to braid straw or hook rugs again, she'd soon be earnin' a little somethin'. An' may be he could do somethin' for Mandy's eyes. They did use to live so neat an' ladylike. Somehow I couldn't speak to tell 'em there that 't was I bought them six best cups an' saucers, time of the auction; they went very low, as everything else did, an' I thought I could save it some other way. They shall have 'em back an' welcome. You're real whole-hearted, Mis' Trimble. I expect Ann 'll be sayin' that her father's child'n wa'n't goin' to be left desolate, an' that all the bread he cast on the water's comin' back through you."

"I don't care what she says, dear creatur'!" exclaimed Mrs. Trimble. "I'm full o' regrets I took time for that installation, an' set there seepin' in a lot o' talk this whole day long, except for its kind of bringin' us to the Bray girls. I wish to my heart 't was to-morrow mornin' a'ready, an' I a-startin' for the selec'*men*."

THE QUEST OF MR. TEABY

The trees were bare on meadow and hill, and all about the country one saw the warm brown of lately fallen leaves. There was still a cheerful bravery of green in sheltered places,—a fine, live green that flattered the eye with its look of permanence; the first three quarters of the year seemed to have worked out their slow processes to make this perfect late-autumn day. In such weather I found even the East Wilby railroad station attractive, and waiting three hours for a slow train became a pleasure; the delight of idleness and even booklessness cannot be properly described.

The interior of the station was bleak and gravelly, but it would have been possible to find fault with any interior on such an out-of-doors day; and after the station-master had locked his ticket-office door and tried the handle twice, with a comprehensive look at me, he went slowly away up the road to spend some leisure time with his family. He had ceased to take any interest in the traveling public, and answered my questions as briefly as possible. After he had gone some distance he turned to look back, but finding that I still sat on the baggage truck in the sunshine, just where he left me, he smothered his natural apprehensions, and went on.

One might spend a good half hour in watching crows as they go southward resolutely through the clear sky, and then waver and come straggling back as if they had forgotten something; one might think over all one's immediate affairs, and learn to know the outward aspect of such a place as East Wilby as if born and brought up there. But after a while I lost interest in both past and future; there was too much landscape before me at the moment, and a lack of figures. The weather was not to be enjoyed merely as an end, yet there was no temptation to explore the up-hill road on the left, or the level fields on the right; I sat still on my baggage truck and waited for something to happen. Sometimes one is so happy that there is nothing left to wish for but to be happier, and just as the remembrance of this truth illuminated my mind, I saw two persons approaching from opposite directions. The first to arrive was a pleasant-looking elderly countrywoman, well wrapped in a worn winter cloak with a thick plaid shawl over it, and a white worsted cloud tied over her bonnet. She carried a well-preserved bandbox,—the outlines were perfect under its checked gingham cover,—and had a large bundle beside, securely rolled in a newspaper. From her dress I felt sure that she had made a mistake in dates, and expected winter to set in at once. Her face was crimson with undue warmth, and what appeared in the end to have been unnecessary haste. She did not take any notice of the elderly man who reached the platform a minute later, until they were near enough to take each other by the hand and exchange most cordial greetings.

"Well, this is a treat!" said the man, who was a small and shivery-looking person. He carried a great umbrella and a thin, enameled-cloth valise, and wore an ancient little silk hat and a nearly new greenish linen duster, as if it were yet summer. "I was full o' thinkin' o' you day before yesterday; strange, wa'n't it?" he announced impressively, in a plaintive voice. "I was sayin' to myself, if there was one livin' bein' I coveted to encounter over East Wilby way, 't was you, Sister Pinkham."

"Warm to-day, ain't it?" responded Sister Pinkham. "How's your health, Mr. Teaby? I guess I'd better set right down here on the aidge of the platform; sha'n't we git more air than if we went inside the depot? It's necessary to git my breath before I rise the hill."

"You can't seem to account for them foresights," continued Mr. Teaby, putting down his tall, thin valise and letting the empty top of it fold over. Then he stood his umbrella against the end of my baggage truck, without a glance at me. I was glad that they were not finding me in their way. "Well, if this ain't very sing'lar, I never saw nothin' that was," repeated the little man. "Nobody can set forth to explain why the thought of you should have been so borne in upon me day before yesterday, your livin' countenance an' all, an' here we be today settin' side o' one another. I've come to rely on them foresights; they've been of consider'ble use in my business, too."

"Trade good as common this fall?" inquired Sister Pinkham languidly. "You don't carry such a thing as a good palm-leaf fan amon'st your stuff, I expect? It does appear to me as if I hadn't been more het up any day this year."

"I should ha' had the observation to offer it before," said Mr. Teaby, with pride. "Yes, Sister Pinkham, I've got an excellent fan right here, an' you shall have it."

He reached for his bag; I heard a clink, as if there were bottles within. Presently his companion began to fan herself with that steady sway and lop of the palm-leaf which one sees only in country churches in midsummer weather. Mr. Teaby edged away a little, as if he feared such a steady trade-wind.

"We might ha' picked out a shadier spot, on your account," he suggested. "Can't you unpin your shawl?"

"Not while I'm so het," answered Sister Pinkham coldly. "Is there anything new recommended for rheumatic complaints?"

"They're gittin' up new compounds right straight along, and sends sights o' printed bills urgin' of me to buy 'em. I don't beseech none o' my customers to take them strange nostrums that I ain't able to recommend."

"Some is new cotches made o' the good old stand-bys, I expect," said Sister Pink-ham, and there was a comfortable silence of some minutes.

"I'm kind of surprised to meet with you to-day, when all's said an' done; it kind of started me when I see 't was you, after dwellin' on you so day before yesterday," insisted Mr. Teaby; and this time Sister Pinkham took heed of the interesting coincidence.

"THINKIN' O' ME, WAS YOU?" and she stopped the fan a moment, and turned to look at him with interest.

"I was so. Well, I never see nobody that kep' her looks as you do, and be'n a sufferer too, as one may express it."

Sister Pinkham sighed heavily, and began to ply the fan again. "You was sayin' just now that you found them foresight notions work into your business."

"Yes'm; I saved a valu'ble life this last spring. I was puttin' up my vials to start out over Briggsville way, an' 't was impressed upon me that I'd better carry a portion o' opodildack. I was loaded up heavy, had all I could lug of spring goods; salts an' seny, and them big-bottle spring bitters o' mine that folks counts on regular. I couldn't git the opodildack out o' my mind noway, and I didn't want it for nothin' nor nobody, but I had to remove a needed vial o' some kind of essence to give it place. When I was goin' down the lane t'wards Abel Dean's house, his women folks come flyin' out. 'Child's a-dyin' in here,' says they; 'tumbled down the sullar stairs.' They was like crazy creatur's; I give 'em the vial right there in the lane, an' they run in an' I followed 'em. Last time I was there the child was a-playin' out; looked rugged and hearty. They've never forgot it an' never will," said Mr. Teaby impressively, with a pensive look toward the horizon. "Want me to stop over night with 'em any time, or come an' take the hoss, or anything. Mis' Dean, she buys four times the essences an' stuff she wants; kind o' gratified, you see, an' didn't want to lose the child, I expect, though she's got a number o' others. If it hadn't be'n for its bein' so impressed on my mind, I should have omitted that opodildack. I deem it a winter remedy, chiefly."

"Perhaps the young one would ha' come to without none; they do survive right through everything, an' then again they seem to be taken away right in their tracks." Sister Pinkham grew more talkative as she cooled. "Heard any news as you come along?"

"Some," vaguely responded Mr. Teaby. "Folks ginerally relates anythin' that's occurred since they see me before. I ain't no great hand for news, an' never was."

"Pity 'bout *you*, Uncle Teaby! There, anybody don't like to have deaths occur an' them things, and be unawares of 'em, an' the last to know when folks calls in." Sister Pinkham laughed at first, but said her say with spirit.

"Certain, certain, we ought all of us to show an interest. I did hear it reported that Elder Fry calculates to give up preachin' an' go into the creamery business another spring. You know he's had means left him, and his throat's kind o' give out; trouble with the pipes. I called it brown caters, an' explained nigh as I could without hurtin' of his pride that he'd bawled more 'n any pipes could stand. I git so wore out settin' under him that I feel to go an' lay right out in the woods arterwards, where it's still. 'T won't never do for him to deal so with callin' of his cows; they'd be so aggravated 't would be more 'n any butter business could bear."

"You hadn't ought to speak so light now; he's a very feelin' man towards any one in trouble," Sister Pinkham rebuked the speaker. "I set consider'ble by Elder Fry. You sort o' divert yourself dallying round the country with your essences and remedies, an' you ain't never sagged down with no settled grievance, as most do. Think o' what the Elder's be'n through, a-losin' o' three good wives. I'm one o' them that ain't found life come none too easy, an' Elder Fry's preachin' stayed my mind consider'ble."

"I s'pose you're right, if you think you be," acknowledged the little man humbly. "I can't say as I esteem myself so fortunate as most. I 'in a lonesome creatur', an' always was; you know I be. I did expect somebody 'd engage my affections before this."

"There, plenty 'd be glad to have ye."

"I expect they would, but I don't seem to be drawed to none on 'em," replied Mr. Teaby, with a mournful shake of his head. "I've spoke pretty decided to quite a number in my time, take 'em all together, but it always appeared best not to follow it up; an' so when I'd come their way again I'd laugh it off or somethin', in case 't was referred to. I see one now an' then that I kind o' fancy, but 't ain't the real thing."

SARAH ORNE JEWETT

"You mustn't expect to pick out a handsome gal, at your age," insisted Sister Pinkham, in a business-like way. "Time's past for all that, an' you've got the name of a rover. I've heard some say that you was rich, but that ain't every thin'. You must take who you can git, and look you up a good home; I would. If you was to be taken down with any settled complaint, you'd be distressed to be without a place o' your own, an' I'm glad to have this chance to tell ye so. Plenty o' folks is glad to take you in for a short spell, an' you've had an excellent chance to look the ground over well. I tell you you're beginnin' to git along in years."

"I know I be," said Mr. Teaby. "I can't travel now as I used to. I have to favor my left leg. I do' know but I be spoilt for settlin' down. This business I never meant to follow stiddy, in the fust place; 't was a means to an end, as one may say."

"Folks would miss ye, but you could take a good long trip, say spring an' fall, an' live quiet the rest of the year. What if they do git out o' essence o' lemon an' pep'mint! There's sufficient to the stores; 't ain't as 't used to be when you begun."

"There's Ann Maria Hart, my oldest sister's daughter. I kind of call it home with her by spells and when the travelin' 's bad."

"Good King Agrippy! if that's the best you can do, I feel for you," exclaimed the energetic adviser. "She's a harmless creatur' and seems to keep ploddin, but slack ain't no description, an' runs on talkin' about nothin' till it strikes right in an' numbs ye. She's pressed for house room, too. Hart ought to put on an addition long ago, but he's too stingy to live. Folks was tellin' me that somebody observed to him how he'd got a real good, stiddy man to work with him this summer. 'He's called a very pious man, too, great hand in meetin's, Mr. Hart,' says they; an' says he, 'I'd have you rec'lect he's a-prayin' out o' my time!' Said it hasty, too, as if he meant it."

"Well, I can put up with Hart; he's near, but he uses me well, an' I try to do the same by him. I don't bange on 'em; I pay my way, an' I feel as if everything was temp'rary. I did plan to go way over North Dexter way, where I've never be'n, an' see if there wa'n't somebody, but the weather ain't be'n settled as I could wish. I'm always expectin' to find her, I be so,"—at which I observed Sister Pinkham's frame shake.

I felt a slight reproach of conscience at listening so intently to these entirely private affairs, and at this point reluctantly left my place and walked along the platform, to remind Sister Pinkham and confiding Mr. Teaby of my neighborhood. They gave no sign that there was any objection to the presence of a stranger, and so I came back gladly to the baggage truck, and we all kept silence for a little while. A fine flavor of extracts was wafted from the valise to where I sat. I pictured to myself the solitary and hopeful wanderings of Mr. Teaby. There was an air about him of some distinction; he might have been a decayed member of the medical profession. I observed that his hands were unhardened by any sort of rural work, and he sat there a meek and appealing figure, with his antique hat and linen duster, beside the well-wadded round shoulders of friendly Sister Pinkham. The expression of their backs was most interesting.

"You might express it that I've got quite a number o' good homes; I've got me sorted out a few regular places where I mostly stop," Mr. Teaby explained presently. "I like to visit with the old folks an' speak o' the past together; an' the boys an' gals, they always have some kind o' fun goin' on when I git along. They always have to git me out to the barn an' tell me, if they're a-courtin', and I fetch an' carry for 'em in that case, an' help out all I can. I've made peace when they got into some o' their misunderstanding, an' them times they set a good deal by Uncle Teaby; but they ain't all got along as well as they expected, and that's be'n one thing that's made me desirous not to git fooled myself. But I do' know as folks would be reconciled to my settlin' down in one place. I've gathered a good many extry receipts for things, an' folks all calls me somethin' of a doctor; you know my grand'ther was one, on my mother's side."

"Well, you've had my counsel for what 't is wuth," said the woman, not unkindly. "Trouble is, you want better bread than's made o' wheat."

"I'm 'most ashamed to ask ye again if 't would be any use to lay the matter before Hannah Jane Pinkham?" This was spoken lower, but I could hear the gentle suggestion.

"I'm obleeged to *you*" said the lady of Mr. Teaby's choice, "but I ain't the right one. Don't you go to settin' your mind on me: 't ain't wuth while. I'm older than you be, an' apt to break down with my rheumatic complaints. You don't want nobody on your hands. I'd git a younger woman, I would so."

"I've be'n a-lookin' for the right one a sight o' years, Hannah Jane. I've had a kind o' notion I should know her right off when I fust see her, but I'm afeared it ain't goin' to be that way. I've seen a sight o' nice, smart women, but when the thought o' you was so impressed on my mind day before yesterday"—

"I'm sorry to disobleege you, but if I have anybody, I'm kind o' half promised to Elder Fry," announced Sister Pinkham bravely. "I consider it more on the off side than I did at first. If he'd continued preachin' I'd favor it more, but I dread havin' to 'tend to a growin' butter business an' to sense them new machines. 'T ain't as if he'd 'stablished it. I've just begun to have things easy; but there, I feel as if I had a lot o' work left in me, an' I don't know's 't is right to let it go to waste. I expect the Elder would preach some, by spells, an' we could ride about an' see folks; an' he'd always be called to funerals, an' have some variety one way an' another. I urge him not to quit preachin'."

"I'd rather he ondertook 'most anythin' else," said Mr. Teaby, rising and trying to find the buttons of his linen duster.

I could see a bitter shade of jealousy cloud his amiable face; but Sister Pinkham looked up at him and laughed. "Set down, set down," she said. "We ain't in no great hurry;" and Uncle Teaby relented, and lingered. "I'm all out o' rose-water for the eyes," she told him, "an' if you've got a vial o' lemon left that you'll part with reasonable, I do' know but I'll take that. I'd rather have caught you when you was outward bound; your bag looks kind o' slim."

"Everythin' 's fresh-made just before I started, 'cept the ginger, an' that I buy, but it's called the best there is."

The two sat down and drove a succession of sharp bargains, but finally parted the best of friends. Mr. Teaby kindly recognized my presence from a business point of view, and offered me a choice of his wares at reasonable prices. I asked about a delightful jumping-jack which made its appearance, and wished very much to become the owner, for it was curiously whittled out and fitted together by Mr. Teaby's own hands. He exhibited the toy to Sister Pinkham and me, to our great pleasure, but scorned to sell such a trifle, it being worth nothing; and beside, he had made it for a little girl who lived two miles farther along the road he was following. I could see that she was a favorite of the old man's, and said no more about the matter, but provided myself, as recommended, with an ample package of court-plaster, "in case of accident before I got to where I was going," and a small bottle of smelling-salts, described as reviving to the faculties.

Then we watched Mr. Teaby plod away, a quaint figure, with his large valise nearly touching the ground as it hung slack from his right hand. The greenish-brown duster looked bleak and unseasonable as a cloud went over the sun; it appeared to symbolize the youthful and spring-like hopes of the wearer, decking the autumn days of life.

"Poor creatur'!" said Sister Pinkham. "There, he doos need somebody to look after him."

She turned to me frankly, and I asked how far he was going.

"Oh, he'll put up at that little gal's house an' git his dinner, and give her the jumpin'-jack an' trade a little; an' then he'll work along the road, callin' from place to place. He's got a good deal o' system, an' was a smart boy, so that folks expected he was goin' to make a doctor, but he kind o' petered out. He's long-winded an' harpin', an' some folks prays him by if they can; but there, most likes him, an' there's nobody would be more missed. He don't make no trouble for 'em; he'll take right holt an' help, and there ain't nobody more gentle with the sick. Always has some o' his nonsense over to me."

This was added with sudden consciousness that I must have heard the recent conversation, but we only smiled at each other, and good Sister Pinkham did not seem displeased. We both turned to look again at the small figure of Mr. Teaby, as he went away, with his queer, tripping gait, along the level road.

"Pretty day, if 't wa'n't quite so warm," said Sister Pinkham, as she rose and reached for her bandbox and bundle, to resume her own journey. "There, if here ain't Uncle Teaby's umbrilla! He forgits everything that belongs to him but that old valise. Folks wouldn't know him if he left that. You may as well just hand it to Asa Briggs, the depot-master, when he gits back. Like's not the old gentleman 'll think to call for it as he comes back along. Here's his fan, too, but he won't be likely to want that this winter."

She looked at the large umbrella; there was a great deal of good material in it, but it was considerably out of repair.

"I don't know but I'll stop an' mend it up for him, poor old creatur'," she said slowly, with an apologetic look at me. Then she sat down again, pulled a large rolled-up needlebook from her deep and accessible pocket, and sewed busily for some time with strong stitches.

I sat by and watched her, and was glad to be of use in chasing her large spool of linen thread, which repeatedly rolled away along the platform. Sister Pinkham's affectionate thoughts were evidently following her old friend.

"I've a great mind to walk back with the umbrilla; he may need it, an' 't ain't a great ways," she said to me, and then looked up quickly, blushing like a girl. I wished she would, for my part, but it did not seem best for a stranger to give advice in such serious business. "I'll tell you what I will do," she told me innocently, a moment afterwards. "I'll take the umbrilla along with me, and leave word with Asa Briggs I've got it. I go right by his house, so you needn't charge your mind nothin' about it."

By the time she had taken off her gold-bowed spectacles and put them carefully away and was ready to make another start, she had learned where I came from and where I was going and what my name was, all this being but poor return for what I had gleaned of the history of herself and Mr. Teaby. I watched Sister Pinkham until she disappeared, umbrella in hand, over the crest of a hill far along the road to the eastward.

THE LUCK OF THE BOGANS

I

The old beggar women of Bantry streets had seldom showered their blessings upon a departing group of emigrants with such hearty good will as they did upon Mike Bogan and his little household one May morning.

Peggy Muldoon, she of the game leg and green-patched eye and limber tongue, steadied herself well back against the battered wall at the street corner and gave her whole energy to a torrent of speech unusual to even her noble powers. She would not let Mike Bogan go to America unsaluted and unblessed; she meant to do full honor to this second cousin, once removed, on the mother's side.

"Yirra, Mike Bogan, is it yerself thin, goyn away beyant the says?" she began with true dramatic fervor. "Let poor owld Peg take her last look on your laughing face me darlin'. She'll be under the ground this time next year, God give her grace, and you far away lavin' to strange spades the worruk of hapin' the sods of her grave. Give me one last look at me darlin' lad wid his swate Biddy an' the shild. Oh that I live to see this day!"

Peg's companions, old Marget Dunn and Biddy O'Hern and no-legged Tom Whinn, the fragment of a once active sailor who propelled himself by a low truckle cart and two short sticks; these interesting members of society heard the shrill note of their leader's eloquence and suddenly appeared like beetles out of unsuspected crevices near by. The side car, upon which Mike Bogan and his wife and child were riding from their little farm outside the town to the place of departure, was stopped at the side of the narrow street. A lank yellow-haired lad, with eyes red from weeping sat swinging his long legs from the car side, another car followed, heavily laden with Mike's sister's family, and a mourning yet envious group of acquaintances footed it in the rear. It was an excited, picturesque little procession; the town was quickly aware of its presence, and windows went up from house to house, and heads came out of the second and third stories and even in the top attics all along the street. The air was thick with blessings, the quiet of Bantry was permanently broken.

"Lard bliss us and save us!" cried Peggy, her shrill voice piercing the chatter and triumphantly lifting itself in audible relief above the din,—"Lard bliss us an' save us for the flower o' Bantry is lavin' us this day. Break my heart wid yer goyn will ye Micky Bogan and make it black night to the one eye that's left in me gray head this fine mornin' o' spring. I that hushed the mother of you and the father of you babies in me arms, and that was a wake old woman followin' and crapin' to see yerself christened. Oh may the saints be good to you Micky Bogan and Biddy Flaherty the wife, and forgive you the sin an' shame of turning yer proud backs on ould Ireland. Ain't there pigs and praties enough for ye in poor Bantry town that her crabbedest childer must lave her. Oh wisha wisha, I'll see your face no more, may the luck o' the Bogans follow you, that failed none o' the Bogans yet. May the sun shine upon you and grow two heads of cabbage in the same sprout, may the little b'y live long and get him a good wife, and if she ain't good to him may she die from him. May every hair on both your heads turn into a blessed candle to light your ways to heaven, but not yit me darlin's—not yit!"

The jaunting car had been surrounded by this time and Mike and his wife were shaking hands and trying to respond impartially to the friendly farewells and blessings of their friends. There never had been such a leave-taking in Bantry. Peggy Muldoon felt that her eloquence was in danger of being ignored and made a final shrill appeal. "Who'll bury me now?" she screamed with a long wail which silenced the whole group; "who'll lay me in the grave, Micky bein' gone from me that always gave me the kind word and the pinny or trippence ivery market day, and the wife of him Biddy Flaherty the rose of Glengariff; many's the fine meal she's put before old Peggy Muldoon that is old and blind."

"Awh, give the ould sowl a pinny now," said a sympathetic voice, "'t will bring you luck, more power to you." And Mike Bogan, the tears streaming down his honest cheeks, plunged deep into his pocket and threw the old beggar a broad five-shilling piece. It was a monstrous fortune to Peggy. Her one eye glared with joy, the jaunting car moved away while she fell flat on the ground in apparent excess of emotion. The farewells were louder for a minute—then they were stopped; the excitable neighborhood returned to its business or idleness and the street was still. Peggy rose rubbing an elbow, and said with the air of a queen to her retinue, "Coom away now poor crathurs, so we'll drink long life to him." And Marget Dunn and Biddy O'Hern and no-legged Tom Whinn with his truckle cart disappeared into an alley.

"What's all this whillalu?" asked a sober-looking, clerical gentleman who came riding by.

"'T is the Bogans going to Ameriky, yer reverence," responded Jim Kalehan, the shoemaker, from his low window. "The folks gived them their wake whilst they were here to enjoy it and them was the keeners that was goin' hippety with lame legs and fine joy down the convanient alley for beer, God bless the poor souls!"

Mike Bogan and Biddy his wife looked behind them again and again. Mike blessed himself fervently as he caught a last glimpse of the old church on the hill where he was christened and married, where his father and his grandfather had been christened and married and buried. He remembered the day when he had first seen his wife, who was there from Glengariff to stay with her old aunt, and coming to early mass, had looked to him like a strange sweet flower abloom on the gray stone pavement where she knelt. The old church had long stood on the steep height at the head of Bantry street and watched and waited for her children. He would never again come in from his little farm in the early morning—he never again would be one of the Bantry men. The golden stories of life in America turned to paltry tinsel, and a love and pride of the old country, never forgotten by her sons and daughters, burned with fierce flame on the inmost altar of his heart. It had all been very easy to dream fine dreams of wealth and landownership, but in that moment the least of the pink daisies that were just opening on the roadside was dearer to the simple-hearted emigrant than all the world beside.

"Lave me down for a bit of sod," he commanded the wondering young driver, who would have liked above all things to sail for the new world. The square of turf from the hedge foot, sparkling with dew and green with shamrock and gay with tiny flowers, was carefully wrapped in Mike's best Sunday handkerchief as they went their way. Biddy had covered her head with her shawl—it was she who had made the plan of going to America, it was she who was eager to join some successful members of her family who had always complained at home of their unjust rent and the difficulties of the crops. Everybody said that the times were going to be harder than ever that summer, and she was quick to catch at the inflammable speeches of some lawless townsfolk who were never satisfied with anything. As for Mike, the times always seemed alike, he did not grudge hard work and he never found fault with the good Irish weather. His nature was not resentful, he only laughed when Biddy assured him that the gorse would soon grow in the thatch of his head as it did on their cabin chimney. It was only when she said that, in America they could make a gentleman of baby

Dan, that the father's blue eyes glistened and a look of determination came into his face.

"God grant we'll come back to it some day," said Mike softly. "I didn't know, faix indeed, how sorry I'd be for lavin' the owld place. Awh Biddy girl 't is many the weary day we'll think of the home we've left," and Biddy removed the shawl one instant from her face only to cover it again and burst into a new shower of tears. The next day but one they were sailing away out of Queenstown harbor to the high seas. Old Ireland was blurring its green and purple coasts moment by moment; Kinsale lay low, and they had lost sight of the white cabins on the hillsides and the pastures golden with furze. Hours before the old women on the wharves had turned away from them shaking their great cap borders. Hours before their own feet had trodden the soil of Ireland for the last time. Mike Bogan and Biddy had left home, they were well on their way to America. Luckily nobody had been with them at last to say good-by—they had taken a more or less active part in the piteous general leave-taking at Queenstown, but those were not the faces of their own mothers or brothers to which they looked back as the ship slid away through the green water.

"Well, sure, we're gone now," said Mike setting his face westward and tramping the steerage deck. "I like the say too, I belave, me own grandfather was a sailor, an' 't is a fine life for a man. Here's little Dan goin' to Ameriky and niver mistrustin'. We'll be sindin' the gossoon back again, rich and fine, to the owld place by and by, 'tis thrue for us, Biddy."

But Biddy, like many another woman, had set great changes in motion and then longed to escape from their consequences. She was much discomposed by the ship's unsteadiness. She accused patient Mike of having dragged her away from home and friends. She grew very white in the face, and was helped to her hard steerage berth where she had plenty of time for reflection upon the vicissitudes of seafaring. As for Mike, he grew more and more enthusiastic day by day over their prospects as he sat in the shelter of the bulkhead and tended little Dan and talked with his companions as they sailed westward.

Who of us have made enough kindly allowance for the homesick quick-witted ambitious Irish men and women, who have landed every year with such high hopes on our shores. There are some of a worse sort, of whom their native country might think itself well rid—but what thrifty New England housekeeper who takes into her home one

SARAH ORNE JEWETT

of the pleasant-faced little captive maids, from Southern Ireland, has half understood the change of surroundings. That was a life in the open air under falling showers and warm sunshine, a life of wit and humor, of lavishness and lack of provision for more than the passing day—of constant companionship with one's neighbors, and a cheerful serenity and lack of nervous anticipation born of the vicinity of the Gulf Stream. The climate makes the characteristics of Cork and Kerry; the fierce energy of the Celtic race in America is forced and stimulated by our own keen air. The beauty of Ireland is little hinted at by an average orderly New England town—many a young girl and many a blundering sturdy fellow is heartsick with the homesickness and restraint of his first year in this golden country of hard work. To so many of them a house has been but a shelter for the night—a sleeping-place: if you remember that, you do not wonder at fumbling fingers or impatience with our houses full of trinkets. Our needless tangle of furnishing bewilders those who still think the flowers that grow of themselves in the Irish thatch more beautiful than anything under the cover of our prosaic shingled roofs.

"Faix, a fellow on deck was telling me a nate story the day," said Mike to Biddy Bogan, by way of kindly amusement. "Says he to me, 'Mike,' says he, 'did ye ever hear of wan Pathrick O'Brien that heard some bla'guard tell how in Ameriky you picked up money in the streets?' 'No,' says I. 'He wint ashore in a place,' says he, 'and he walked along and he come to a sign on a wall. Silver Street was on it. "I 'ont stap here," says he, "it ain't wort my while at all, at all. I'll go on to Gold Street," says he, but he walked ever since and he ain't got there yet.'"

Biddy opened her eyes and laughed feebly. Mike looked so bronzed and ruddy and above all so happy, that she took heart. "We're sound and young, thanks be to God, and we'll earn an honest living," said Mike, proudly. "'T is the childher I'm thinkin' of all the time, an' how they'll get a chance the best of us niver had at home. God bless old Bantry forever in spite of it. An' there's a smart rid-headed man that has every bother to me why 'ont I go with him and keep a tidy bar. He's been in the same business this four year gone since he come out, and twenty pince in his pocket when he landed, and this year he took a month off and went over to see the ould folks and build 'em a dacint house intirely, and hire a man to farm wid 'em now the old ones is old. He says will I put in my money wid him, an he'll give me a great start I wouldn't have in three years else."

"Did you have the fool's head on you then and let out to him what manes you had?" whispered Biddy, fiercely and lifting herself to look at him.

"I did then; 't was no harm," answered the unsuspecting Mike.

"'T was a black-hearted rascal won the truth from you!" and Biddy roused her waning forces and that very afternoon appeared on deck. The red-headed man knew that he had lost the day when he caught her first scornful glance.

"God pity the old folks of him an' their house," muttered the sharp-witted wife to Mike, as she looked at the low-lived scheming fellow whom she suspected of treachery.

"He said thim was old clothes he was wearin' on the sea," apologized Mike for his friend, looking down somewhat consciously at his own comfortable corduroys. He and Biddy had been well to do on their little farm, and on good terms with their landlord the old squire. Poor old gentleman, it had been a sorrow to him to let the young people go. He was a generous, kindly old man, but he suffered from the evil repute of some shortsighted neighbors. "If I gave up all I had in the world and went to the almshouse myself, they would still damn me for a landlord," he said, desperately one day. "But I never thought Mike Bogan would throw up his good chances. I suppose some worthless fellow called him stick-in-the-mud and off he must go."

There was some unhappiness at first for the young people in America. They went about the streets of their chosen town for a day or two, heavy-hearted with disappointment. Their old neighbors were not housed in palaces after all, as the letters home had suggested, and after a few evenings of visiting and giving of messages, and a few days of aimless straying about, Mike and Biddy hired two rooms at a large rent up three flights of stairs, and went to housekeeping. Litte Dan rolled down one flight the first day; no more tumbling on the green turf among the daisies for him, poor baby boy. His father got work at the forge of a carriage shop, having served a few months with a smith at home, and so taking rank almost as a skilled laborer. He was a great favorite speedily, his pay was good, at least it would have been good if he had lived on the old place among the fields, but he and Biddy did not know how to make the most of it here, and Dan had a baby sister presently to keep him company, and then another and another, and there they lived up-stairs in the heat, in the cold, in daisy time and snow time, and Dan was put to school and came home with a knowledge of sums in arithmetic which set his father's eyes dancing with delight, but with a knowledge besides of foul language and a brutal way of treating his little sisters when nobody was looking on.

Mike Bogan was young and strong when he came to America, and his good red blood lasted well, but it was against his nature to work in a hot half-lighted shop, and in a very few years he began to look pale about the mouth and shaky in the shoulders, and then the enthusiastic promises of the red-headed man on the ship, borne out, we must allow, by Mike's own observation, inclined him and his hard earned capital to the purchase of a tidy looking drinking shop on a side street of the town. The owner had died and his widow wished to go West to live with her son. She knew the Bogans and was a respectable soul in her way. She and her husband had kept a quiet place, everybody acknowledged, and everybody was thankful that since drinking shops must be kept, so decent a man as Mike Bogan was taking up the business.

II

The luck of the Bogans proved to be holding true in this generation. Their proverbial good fortune seemed to come rather from an absence of bad fortune than any special distinction granted the generation or two before Mike's time. The good fellow sometimes reminded himself gratefully of Peggy Muldoon's blessing, and once sent her a pound to keep Christmas upon. If he had only known it, that unworthy woman bestowed curses enough upon him because he did not repeat it the next year, to cancel any favors that might have been anticipated. Good news flew back to Bantry of his prosperity, and his comfortable home above the store was a place of reception and generous assistance to all the westward straying children of Bantry. There was a bit of garden that belonged to the estate, the fences were trig and neat, and neither Mike nor Biddy were persons to let things look shabby while they had plenty of money to keep them clean and whole. It was Mike who walked behind the priest on Sundays when the collection was taken. It was Mike whom good Father Miles trusted more than any other member of his flock, whom he confided in and consulted, whom perhaps his reverence loved best of all the parish because they were both Bantry men, born and bred. And nobody but Father Miles and Biddy and Mike Bogan knew the full extent of the father's and mother's pride and hope in the cleverness and beauty of their only son. Nothing was too great, and no success seemed impossible when they tried to picture the glorious career of little Dan.

Mike was a kind father to his little daughters, but all his hope was for Dan. It was for Dan that he was pleased when people called him Mr. Bogan in respectful tones, and when he was given a minor place of trust at town elections, he thought with humble gladness that Dan would have less cause to be ashamed of him by and by when he took his own place as gentleman and scholar. For there was something different about Dan from the rest of them, plain Irish folk that they were. Dan was his father's idea of a young lord; he would have liked to show the boy to the old squire, and see his look of surprise. Money came in at the shop door in a steady stream, there was plenty of it put away in the bank and Dan must wear well-made clothes and look like the best fellows at the school. He was handsomer than any of them, he was the best and quickest scholar of his class. The president of the great carriage company had said that he was a very promising boy more than once, and had put his hand on Mike's shoulder as he spoke. Mike and Biddy, dressed in their best, went to the school examinations year after year and heard their son do better than the rest, and saw him noticed and admired. For Dan's sake no noisy men were allowed to stay about the shop. Dan himself was forbidden to linger there, and so far the boy had clear honest eyes, and an affectionate way with his father that almost broke that honest heart with joy. They talked together when they went to walk on Sundays, and there was a plan, increasingly interesting to both, of going to old Bantry some summer—just for a treat. Oh happy days! They must end as summer days do, in winter weather.

There was an outside stair to the two upper stories where the Bogans lived above their place of business, and late one evening, when the shop shutters were being clasped together below, Biddy Bogan heard a familiar heavy step and hastened to hold her brightest lamp in the doorway.

"God save you," said his reverence Father Miles, who was coming up slowly, and Biddy dropped a decent courtesy and devout blessing in return. His reverence looked pale and tired, and seated himself wearily in a chair by the window—while Biddy coasted round by a bedroom door to "whist" at two wakeful daughters who were teasing each other and chattering in bed.

"'T is long since we saw you here, sir," she said, respectfully. "'T is warm weather indade for you to be about the town, and folks sick an' dyin' and needing your help, sir. Mike'll be up now, your reverence. I hear him below."

Biddy had grown into a stout mother of a family, red-faced and bustling; there was little likeness left to the rose of Glengariff with whom Mike had fallen in love at early mass in Bantry church. But the change had been so gradual that Mike himself had never become conscious of any damaging difference. She took a fresh loaf of bread and cut some generous slices and put a piece of cheese and a knife on the table within reach of Father Miles's hand. "I suppose 'tis waste of time to give you more, so it is," she said to him. "Bread an' cheese and no better will you ate I suppose, sir," and she folded her arms across her breast and stood looking at him.

"How is the luck of the Bogans to-day?" asked the kind old man. "The head of the school I make no doubt?" and at this moment Mike came up the stairs and greeted his priest with reverent affection.

"You're looking faint, sir," he urged. "Biddy get a glass now, we're quite by ourselves sir—and I've something for sickness that's very soft and fine entirely."

"Well, well, this once then," answered Father Miles, doubtfully. "I've had a hard day."

He held the glass in his hand for a moment and then pushed it away from him on the table. "Indeed it's not wrong in itself," said the good priest looking up presently, as if he had made something clear to his mind. "The wrong is in ourselves to make beasts of ourselves with taking too much of it. I don't shame me with this glass of the best that you've poured for me. My own sin is in the coffee-pot. It wilds my head when I've got most use for it, and I'm sure of an aching pate—God forgive me for indulgence; but I must have it for my breakfast now, and then. Give me a bit of bread and cheese; yes, that's what I want Bridget," and he pushed the glass still farther away.

"I've been at a sorry place this night," he went on a moment later, "the smell of the stuff can't but remind me. 'T is a comfort to come here and find your house so clean and decent, and both of you looking me in the face. God save all poor sinners!" and Mike and his wife murmured assent.

"I wish to God you were out of this business and every honest man with you," said the priest, suddenly dropping his fatherly, Bantry good fellowship and making his host conscious of the solemnity of the church altar. "'T is a decent shop you keep, Mike, my lad, I know. I know no harm of it, but there are weak souls that can't master themselves, and the drink drags them down. There's little use in doing away with the shops though. We've got to make young men strong enough to let drink alone. The drink will always be in the world. Here's your bright young son; what are they teaching him at his school, do ye know? Has his characther grown, do ye think Mike Bogan, and is he going to be a man for good, and to help decent things get a start and bad things to keep their place? I don't care how he does his sums, so I don't, if he has no characther, and they may fight about beer and fight about temperance and carry their Father Matthew flags flying high, so they may, and it's all no good, lessen we can raise the young folks up above the place where drink and shame can touch them. God grant us help," he whispered, dropping his head on his breast. "I'm getting to be an old man myself, and I've never known the temptation that's like a hounding devil to many men. I can let drink alone, God pity those who can't.

Keep the young lads out from it Mike. You're a good fellow, you're careful, but poor human souls are weak, God knows!"

"'T is thrue for you indade sir!" responded Biddy. Her eyes were full of tears at Father Miles's tone and earnestness, but she could not have made clear to herself what he had said.

"Will I put a dhrap more of wather in it, your riverence?" she suggested, but the priest shook his head gently, and, taking a handful of parish papers out of his pocket, proceeded to hold conference with the master of the house. Biddy waited a while and at last ventured to clear away the good priest's frugal supper. She left the glass, but he went away without touching it, and in the very afterglow of his parting blessing she announced that she had the makings of a pain within, and took the cordial with apparent approval.

Mike did not make any comment; he was tired and it was late, and long past their bedtime.

Biddy was wide awake and talkative from her tonic, and soon pursued the subject of conversation.

"What set the father out wid talking I do' know?" she inquired a little ill-humoredly. "'T was thrue for him that we kape a dacint shop anyhow, an' how will it be in the way of poor Danny when it's finding the manes to put him where he is?"

"'T wa'n't that he mint at all," answered Mike from his pillow. "Didn't ye hear what he said?" after endeavoring fruitlessly to repeat it in his own words—"He's right, sure, about a b'y's getting thim books and having no charácther. He thinks well of Danny, and he knows no harm of him. Wisha! what 'll we do wid that b'y, Biddy, I do' know! 'Fadther,' says he to me today, 'why couldn't ye wait an' bring me into the wurruld on American soil,' says he 'and maybe I'd been prisident,' says he, and 't was the thruth for him."

"I'd rather for him to be a priest meself," replied the mother.

"That's what Father Miles said himself the other day," announced Mike wide awake now. "'I wish he'd the makings of a good priest,' said he. 'There'll soon be need of good men and hard picking for 'em too,' said he, and he let a great sigh. ''T is money they want and place they want, most o' them bla'guard b'ys in the siminary. 'T is the old fashioned min like mesilf that think however will they get souls through this life and through heaven's gate at last, wid clane names and God-fearin', dacint names left after them.' Thim was his own words indade."

"Idication was his cry always," said Bridget, blessing herself in the dark. "'T was only last confission he took no note of me own sins while he redded himself in the face with why don't I kape Mary Ellen to the school, and myself not an hour in the day to rest my poor bones. 'I have to kape her in, to mind the shmall childer,' says I, an' 't was thrue for me, so it was." She gave a jerk under the blankets, which represented the courtesy of the occasion. She had a great respect and some awe for Father Miles, but she considered herself to have held her ground in that discussion.

"We'll do our best by them all, sure," answered Mike. "'T is tribbling me money I am ivery day," he added, gayly. "The lord-liftinant himsilf is no surer of a good bury-in' than you an' me. What if we made a priest of Dan intirely?" with a great outburst of proper pride. "A son of your own at the alther saying mass for you, Biddy Flaherty from Glengariff!"

"He's no mind for it, more's the grief," answered the mother, unexpectedly, shaking her head gloomily on the pillow, "but marruk me wuds now, he'll ride in his carriage when I'm under the sods, give me grace and you too Mike Bogan! Look at the airs of him and the toss of his head. 'Mother,' says he to me, 'I'm goin' to be a big man!' says he, 'whin I grow up. D' ye think anybody 'll take me fer an Irishman?'"

"Bad cess to the bla'guard fer that then!" said Mike. "It's spoilin' him you are. 'T is me own pride of heart to come from old Bantry, an' he lied to me yesterday gone, saying would I take him to see the old place. Wisha! he's got too much tongue, and he's spindin' me money for me."

But Biddy pretended to be falling asleep. This was not the first time that the honest pair had felt anxiety creeping into their pride about Dan. He frightened them sometimes; he was cleverer than they, and the mother had already stormed at the boy for his misdemeanors, in her garrulous fashion, but covered them from his father notwithstanding. She felt an assurance of the merely temporary damage of wild oats; she believed it was just as well for a boy to have his freedom and his fling. She even treated his known lies as if they were truth. An easy-going comfortable soul was Biddy, who with much shrewdness and only a trace of shrewishness got through this evil world as best she might.

The months flew by. Mike Bogan was a middle-aged man, and he and his wife looked somewhat elderly as they went to their pew in the broad aisle on Sunday morning. Danny usually came too, and the girls, but Dan looked contemptuous as he sat next his father and said his prayers perfunctorily. Sometimes he was not there at all, and Mike had a heavy heart under his stiff best coat. He was richer than any other member of Father Miles's parish, and he was known and respected everywhere as a good citizen. Even the most ardent believers in the temperance cause were known to say that little mischief would be done if all the rumsellers were such men as Mr. Bogan. He was generous and in his limited way public spirited. He did his duty to his neighbor as he saw it. Every one used liquor more or less, somebody must sell it, but a low groggery was as much a thing of shame to him as to any man. He never sold to boys, or to men who had had too much already. His shop was clean and wholesome, and in the evening when a dozen or more of his respectable acquaintances gathered after work for a social hour or two and a glass of whiskey to rest and cheer them after exposure, there was not a little good talk about affairs from their point of view, and plenty of honest fun. In their own houses very likely the rooms were close and hot, and the chairs hard and unrestful. The wife had taken her bit of recreation by daylight and visited her friends. This was their comfortable club-room, Mike Bogan's shop, and Mike himself the leader of the assembly. There was a sober-mindedness in the man; his companions were contented though he only looked on tolerantly at their fun, for the most part, without taking any active share himself.

One cool October evening the company was well gathered in, there was even a glow of wood fire in the stove, and two of the old men were sitting close beside it. Corny Sullivan had been a soldier in the British army for many years, he had been wounded at last at Sebastopol, and yet here he was, full of military lore and glory, and propped by a wooden leg. Corny was usually addressed an Timber-toes by his familiars; he was an irascible old follow to deal with, but as clean as a whistle from long habit and even stately to look at in his arm-chair. He had a nephew with whom he made his home, who would give him an arm presently and get him home to bed. His mate was an old sailor much bent in the back by rheumatism, Jerry Bogan; who, though no relation, was tenderly treated by Mike, being old and poor. His score was never kept, but he seldom wanted for his evening grog. Jerry Bogan was a cheerful soul; the wit of the Celts and their pathetic wilfulness were delightful in him. The priest liked him, the doctor half loved him, this old-fashioned Irishman who had a graceful compliment or a thrust of wit for whoever came in his way. What a treasury of old Irish lore and legend was this old sailor! What broadness and good cheer and charity had been fostered in his sailor heart! The delight of little children with his clever tales and mysterious performances with bits of soft pine and a sharp jackknife, a very Baron Munchausen of adventure, and here he sat, round backed and head pushed forward like an old turtle, by the fire. The other men sat or stood about the low-walled room. Mike was serving his friends; there was a clink of glass and a stirring and shaking, a pungent odor of tobacco, and much laughter.

"Soombody, whoiver it was, thrun a cat down in Tom Auley's well las' night," announced Corny Sullivan with more than usual gravity.

"They'll have no luck thin," says Jerry. "Anybody that meddles wid wather 'ill have no luck while they live, faix they 'ont thin."

"Tom Auley's been up watchin' this three nights now," confides the other old gossip. "Thim dirty b'y's troublin' his pigs in the sthy, and having every stramash about the place, all for revenge upon him for gettin' the police afther thim when they sthole his hins. 'T was as well for him too, they're dirty bligards, the whole box and dice of them."

"Whishper now!" and Jerry pokes his great head closer to his friend. "The divil of 'em all is young Dan Bogan, Mike's son. Sorra a bit o' good is all his schoolin', and Mike's heart 'll be soon broke from him. I see him goin' about wid his nose in the air. He's a pritty boy, but the divil is in him an' 't is he ought to have been a praste wid his chances and Father Miles himself tarkin and tarkin wid him tryin' to make him a crown of pride to his people after all they did for him. There was niver a spade in his hand to touch the ground yet. Look at his poor father now! Look at Mike, that's grown old and gray since winther time." And they turned their eyes to the bar to refresh their memories with the sight of the disappointed face behind it.

There was a rattling at the door-latch just then and loud voices outside, and as the old men looked, young Dan Bogan came stumbling into the shop. Behind him were two low fellows, the worst in the town, they had all been drinking more than was good for them, and for the first time Mike Bogan saw his only son's boyish face reddened and stupid with whiskey. It had been an unbroken law that Dan should keep out of the shop with his comrades; now he strode forward with an absurd travesty of manliness, and demanded liquor for himself and his friends at his father's hands.

Mike staggered, his eyes glared with anger. His fatherly pride made him long to uphold the poor boy before so many witnesses. He reached for a glass, then he pushed it away—and with quick step reached Dan's side, caught him by the collar, and held him. One or two of the spectators chuckled with weak excitement, but the rest pitied Mike Bogan as he would have pitied them.

The angry father pointed his son's companions to the door, and after a moment's hesitation they went skulking out, and father and son disappeared up the stairway. Dan was a coward, he was glad to be thrust into his own bedroom upstairs, his head was dizzy, and he muttered only a feeble oath. Several of Mike Bogan's customers had kindly disappeared when he returned trying to look the same as ever, but one after another the great tears rolled down his cheeks. He never had faced despair till now; he turned his back to the men, and fumbled aimlessly among the bottles on the shelf. Some one came, in unconscious of the pitiful scene, and impatiently repeated his order to the shopkeeper.

"God help me, boys, I can't sell more this night!" he said brokenly. "Go home now and lave me to myself."

They were glad to go, though it cut the evening short. Jerry Bogan bundled his way last with his two canes. "Sind the b'y to say," he advised in a gruff whisper. "Sind him out wid a good captain now, Mike, 't will make a man of him yet."

A man of him yet! alas, alas—for the hopes that had been growing so many years. Alas for the pride of a simple heart, alas for the day Mike Bogan came away from sunshiny old Bantry with his baby son in his arms for the sake of making that son a gentleman.

III

Winter had fairly set in, but the snow had not come, and the street was bleak and cold. The wind was stinging men's faces and piercing the wooden houses. A hard night for sailors coming on the coast—a bitter night for poor people everywhere.

From one house and another the lights went out in the street where the Bogans lived; at last there was no other lamp than theirs, in a window that lighted the outer stairs. Sometimes a woman's shadow passed across the curtain and waited there, drawing it away from the panes a moment as if to listen the better for a footstep that did not come. Poor Biddy had waited many a night before this. Her husband was far from well, the doctor said that his heart was not working right, and that he must be very careful, but the truth was that Mike's heart was almost broken by grief. Dan was going the downhill road, he had been drinking harder and harder, and spending a great deal of money. He had smashed more than one carriage and lamed more than one horse from the livery stables, and he had kept the lowest company in vilest dens. Now he threatened to go to New York, and it had come at last to being the only possible joy that he should come home at any time of night rather than disappear no one knew where. He had laughed in Father Miles's face when the good old man, after pleading with him, had tried to threaten him.

Biddy was in an agony of suspense as the night wore on. She dozed a little only to wake with a start, and listen for some welcome sound out in the cold night. Was her boy freezing to death somewhere? Other mothers only scolded if their sons were wild, but this was killing her and Mike, they had set their hopes so high. Mike was groaning dreadfully in his sleep to-night—the fire was burning low, and she did not dare to stir it. She took her worn rosary again and tried to tell its beads. "Mother of Pity, pray for us!" she said, wearily dropping the beads in her lap.

There was a sound in the street at last, but it was not of one man's stumbling feet, but of many. She was stiff with cold, she had slept long, and it was almost day. She rushed with strange apprehension to the doorway and stood with the flaring lamp in her hand at the top of the stairs. The voices were suddenly hushed. "Go for Father Miles!" said somebody in a hoarse voice, and she heard the words. They were carrying a burden, they brought it tip to the mother who waited. In their arms lay her son stone dead; he had been stabbed in a fight, he had struck a man down who had sprung back at him like a tiger. Dan, little Dan, was dead, the luck of the Bogans, the end was here, and a wail that pierced the night, and chilled the hearts that heard it, was the first message of sorrow to the poor father in his uneasy sleep.

The group of men stood by—some of them had been drinking, but they were all awed and shocked. You would have believed every one of them to be on the side of law and order. Mike Bogan knew that the worst had happened. Biddy had rushed to him and fallen across the bed; for one minute her aggravating shrieks had stopped; he began to dress himself, but he was shaking too much; he stepped out to the kitchen and faced the frightened crowd.

"Is my son dead, then?" asked Mike Bogan of Bantry, with a piteous quiver of the lip, and nobody spoke. There was something glistening and awful about his pleasant Irish face. He tottered where he stood, he caught at a chair to steady himself. "The luck o' the Bogans is it?" and he smiled strangely, then a fierce hardness came across his face and changed it utterly. "Come down, come down!" he shouted, and snatching the key of the shop went down the stairs himself with great sure-footed leaps. What was in Mike? was he crazy with grief? They stood out of his way and saw him fling out bottle after bottle and shatter them against the wall. They saw him roll one cask after another to the doorway, and out into the street in the gray light of morning, and break through the staves with a heavy axe. Nobody dared to restrain his fury—there was a devil in him, they were afraid of the man in his blinded rage The odor of whiskey and gin filled the cold air—some of them would have stolen the wasted liquor if they could, but no man there dared to move or speak, and it was not until the tall figure of Father Miles came along the street, and the patient eyes that seemed always to keep vigil, and the calm voice with its flavor of Bantry brogue, came to Mike Bogan's help, that he let himself be taken out of the wrecked shop and away from the spilt liquors to the shelter of his home.

A week later he was only a shadow of his sturdy self, he was lying on his bed dreaming of Bantry Bay and the road to Glengariff—the hedge roses were in bloom, and he was trudging along the road to see Biddy. He was working on the old farm at home and could not put the seed potatoes in their trench, for little Dan kept falling in and getting in his way. "Dan's not going to be plagued with the bad craps," he muttered to Father Miles who sat beside the bed. "Dan will be a fine squire in

Ameriky," but the priest only stroked his hand as it twitched and lifted on the coverlet. What was Biddy doing, crying and putting the candles about him? Then Mike's poor brain grew steady.

"Oh, my God, if we were back in Bantry! I saw the gorse bloomin' in the t'atch d' ye know. Oh wisha wisha the poor ould home an' the green praties that day we come from it—with our luck smilin' us in the face."

"Whist darlin': kape aisy darlin'!" mourned Biddy, with a great sob. Father Miles sat straight and stem in his chair by the pillow—he had said the prayers for the dying, and the holy oil was already shining on Mike Bogan's forehead. The keeners were swaying themselves to and fro, there where they waited in the next room.

FAIR DAY

W idow Mercy Bascom came back alone into the empty kitchen and seated herself in her favorite splint-bottomed chair by the window, with a dreary look on her face.

"I s'pose I be an old woman, an' past goin' to cattle shows an' junketings, but folks needn't take it so for granted. I'm sure I don't want to be on my feet all day, trapesin' fair grounds an' swallowin' everybody's dust; not but what I'm as able as most, though I be seventy-three year old."

She folded her hands in her lap and looked out across the deserted yard. There was not even a hen in sight; she was left alone for the day. "Tobias's folks," as she called the son's family with whom she made her home—Tobias's folks had just started for a day's pleasuring at the county fair, ten miles distant. She had not thought of going with them, nor expected any invitation; she had even helped them off with her famous energy; but there was an unexpected reluctance at being left behind, a sad little feeling that would rise suddenly in her throat as she stood in the door and saw them drive away in the shiny, two-seated wagon. Johnny, the youngest and favorite of her grandchildren, had shouted back in his piping voice, "I wish you was goin', Grandma."

"The only one on 'em that thought of me," said Mercy Bascom to herself, and then not being a meditative person by nature, she went to work industriously and proceeded to the repairing of Tobias's work-day coat. It was sharp weather now in the early morning, and he would soon need the warmth of it. Tobias's placid wife never anticipated and always lived in a state of trying to catch up with her work. It never had been the elder woman's way, and Mercy reviewed her own active career with no mean pride. She had been left a widow at twenty-eight, with four children and a stony New Hampshire farm, but had bravely won her way, paid her debts, and provided the three girls and their brother Tobias with the best available schooling.

For a woman of such good judgment and high purpose in life, Mrs. Bascom had made a very unwise choice in marrying Tobias Bascom the elder. He was not even the owner of a good name, and led her a terrible life with his drunken shiftlessness, and hindrance of all her own better aims. Even while the children were babies, however, and life was at its busiest and most demanding stages, the determined soul would not be baffled by such damaging partnership. She showed the plainer of what stuff she was made, and simply worked the harder and went her ways more fiercely. If it were sometimes whispered that she was unamiable, her wiser neighbors understood the power of will that was needed to cope with circumstances that would have crushed a weaker woman. As for her children, they were very fond of her in the undemonstrative New England fashion. Only the two eldest could remember their father at all, and after he was removed from this world Tobias Bascom left but slight proofs of having ever existed at all, except in the stern lines and premature aging of his wife's face.

The years that followed were years of hard work on the little farm, but diligence and perseverance had their reward. When the three daughters came to womanhood they were already skilled farmhouse keepers, and were dispatched for their own homes well equipped with feather-beds and homespun linen and woolen. Mercy Bascom was glad to have them well settled, if the truth were known. She did not like to have her own will and law questioned or opposed, and when she sat down to supper alone with her son Tobias, after the last daughter's wedding, she had a glorious feeling of peace and satisfaction.

"There's a sight o' work left yet in the old ma'am," she said to Tobias, in an unwontedly affectionate tone. "I guess we shall keep house together as comfortable as most folks." But Tobias grew very red in the face and bent over his plate.

"I don' know's I want the girls to get ahead of me," he said sheepishly. "I ain't meanin' to put you out with another wedding right away, but I've been a-lookin' round, an' I guess I've found somebody to suit *me*."

Mercy Bascom turned cold with misery and disappointment. "Why T'bias," she said, anxiously, "folks always said that you was cut out for an old bachelor till I come to believe it, an' I've been lottin' on"—

"Course nobody's goin' to wrench me an' you apart," said Tobias gallantly. "I made up my mind long ago you an' me was yoke-mates, mother. An' I had it in my mind to fetch you somebody that would ease you o' quite so much work now 'Liza's gone off."

"I don't want nobody," said the grieved woman, and she could eat no more supper; that festive supper for which she had cooked her very best. Tobias was sorry for her, but he had his rights, and now simply felt light-hearted because he had freed his mind of this unwelcome declaration. Tobias was slow and stolid to behold, but he was a man of sound ideas and great talent for farming. He had found it difficult to choose between his favorites among the marriageable girls, a bright young creature who was really too good for him, but penniless, and a weaker damsel who was heiress to the best farm in town. The farm won the day at last; and Mrs. Bascom felt a thrill of pride at her son's worldly success; then she asked to know her son's plans, and was wholly disappointed. Tobias meant to sell the old place; he had no idea of leaving her alone as she wistfully complained; he meant to have her make a new home at the Bassett place with him and his bride.

That she would never do: the old place which had given them a living never should be left or sold to strangers. Tobias was not prepared for her fierce outburst of reproach at the mere suggestion. She would live alone and pay her way as she always had done, and so it was, for a few years of difficulties. Tobias was never ready to plough or plant when she needed him; his own great farm was more than he could serve properly. It grew more and more difficult to hire workmen, and they were seldom worth their wages. At last Tobias's wife, who was a kindly soul, persuaded her reluctant mother-in-law to come and spend a winter; the old woman was tired and for once disheartened; she found herself deeply in love with her grandchildren, and so next spring she let the little hill farm on the halves to an impecunious but hard-working young couple.

To everybody's surprise the two women lived together harmoniously. Tobias's wife did everything to please her mother-in-law except to be other than a Bassett. And Mercy, for the most part, ignored this misfortune, and rarely was provoked into calling it a fault. Now that the necessity for hard work and anxiety was past, she appeared to have come to an Indian summer shining-out of her natural amiability and tolerance. She was sometimes indirectly reproachful of her daughter's easy-going ways, and set an indignant example now and then by a famous onslaught of unnecessary work, and always dressed and behaved herself in plainest farm fashion, while Mrs. Tobias was given to undue worldliness and style. But they worked well together in the main, for, to use Mercy's own words, she "had seen enough of life not to want to go into other folks' houses and make trouble."

As people grow older their interests are apt to become fewer, and one of the thoughts that came oftenest to Mercy Bascom in her old age was a time-honored quarrel with one of her husband's sisters, who had been her neighbor many years before, and then moved to greater prosperity at the other side of the county. It is not worth while to tell the long story of accusations and misunderstandings, but while the two women did not meet for almost half a lifetime the grievance was as fresh as if it were yesterday's. Wrongs of defrauded sums of money and contested rights in unproductive acres of land, wrongs of slighting remarks and contempt of equal claims; the remembrance of all these was treasured as a miser fingers his gold. Mercy Bascom freed herself from the wearisome detail of every-day life whenever she could find a patient listener to whom to tell the long story. She found it as interesting as a story of the Arabian Nights, or an exciting play at the theatre. She would have you believe that she was faultless in the matter, and would not acknowledge that her sister-in-law Ruth Bascom, now Mrs. Parlet, was also a hard-working woman with dependent little children at the time of the great fray. Of late years her son had suspected that his mother regretted the alienation, but he knew better than to suggest a peace-making. "Let them work—let them work!" he told his wife, when she proposed one night to bring the warring sisters-in-law unexpectedly together. It may have been that old Mercy began to feel a little lonely and would be glad to have somebody of her own age with whom to talk over old times. She never had known the people much in this Bassett region, and there were few but young folks left at any rate.

As the pleasure-makers hastened toward the fair that bright October morning Mercy sat by the table sewing at a sufficient patch in the old coat. There was little else to do all day but to get herself a luncheon at noon and have supper ready when the family came home cold and tired at night. The two cats came purring about her chair; one persuaded her to open the cellar door, and the other leaped to the top of the kitchen table unrebuked, and blinked herself to sleep there in the sun. This was a favored kitten brought from the old home, and seemed like a link between the old days and these. Her mistress noticed with surprise that pussy was beginning to look old, and she could not resist a little sigh. "Land! the next world may seem dreadful new too, and I've got to get used to that," she thought with a grim smile of foreboding. "How do folks live that wants always to be on the go? There was Ruth Parlet, that must be always a visitin' and goin'—well, I won't say that there wasn't a time when I wished for the chance." Justice always won the day in such minor questions as this.

Ruth Parlet's name started the usual thoughts, but somehow or other Mercy could not find it in her heart to be as harsh as usual. She remembered one thing after another about their girlhood together. They had been great friends then, and the animosity may have had its root in the fact that Ruth helped forward her brother's marriage. But there were years before that of friendly foregathering and girlish alliances and rivalries; spinning and herb gathering and quilting. It seemed, as Mercy thought about it, that Ruth was good company after all. But what did make her act so, and turn right round later on?

The morning grew warm, and at last Mrs. Bascom had to open the window to let out the buzzing flies and an imprisoned wild bee. The patch was finished and the elbow would serve Tobias as good as new. She laid the coat over a chair and put her bent brass thimble into the paper-collar box that served as work-basket. She used to have a queer splint basket at the old place, but it had been broken under something heavier when her household goods were moved. Some of the family had long been tired of hearing that basket regretted, and another had never been found worthy to take its place. The thimble, the smooth mill bobbin on which was wound black linen thread, the dingy lump of beeswax, and a smart leather needle-book, which Johnny had given her the Christmas before, all looked ready for use, but Mrs. Bascom pushed them farther back on the table and quickly rose to her feet. "'T ain't nine o'clock yet," she said, exultantly. "I'll just take a couple o' crackers in my pocket and step over to the old place. I'll take my time and be back soon enough to make 'em that pan o' my hot gingerbread they'll be counting on for supper."

Half an hour later one might have seen a bent figure lock the side door of the large farmhouse carefully, trying the latch again and again to see if it were fast, putting the key into a safe hiding-place by the door, and then stepping away up the road with eager determination. "I ain't felt so like a jaunt this five year," said Mercy to herself, "an' if Tobias was here an' Ann, they'd take all the fun out fussin' and talkin', an' bein' afeard I'd tire myself, or wantin' me to ride over. I do like to be my own master once in a while."

The autumn day was glorious, with a fine flavor of fruit and ripeness in the air. The sun was warm, there was a cool breeze from the great hills, and far off across the wide valley the old woman could see her little gray house on its pleasant eastern slope; she could even trace the outline of the two small fields and large pasture. "I done well with it, if I wasn't nothin' but a woman with four dependin' on me an' no means," said Mercy proudly as she came in full sight of the old place. It was a long drive from one farm to the other by roundabout highways, but there was a footpath known to the wayfarer which took a good piece off the distance. "Now, ain't this a sight better than them hustlin' fairs?" Mercy asked gleefully as she felt herself free and alone in the wide meadow-land. She had long been promising little Johnny to take him over to Gran'ma's house, as she loved to call it still. She could not help thinking longingly how much he would enjoy this escapade. "Why, I'm running away just like a young-one, that's what I be," she exclaimed, and then laughed aloud for very pleasure.

The weather-beaten farmhouse was deserted that day, as its former owner suspected. She boldly gathered some of her valued spice-apples, with an assuring sense of proprietorship as she crossed the last narrow field. The Browns, man and wife and little boy and baby, had hied them early to the fair with nearly the whole population of the countryside. The house and yard and out-buildings never had worn such an aspect of appealing pleasantness as when Mercy Bascom came near. She felt as if she were going to cry for a minute, and then hurried to get inside the gate. She saw the outgoing track of horses' feet with delight, but went discreetly to the door and knocked, to make herself perfectly sure that there was no one left at home. Out of breath and tired as she was, she turned to look off at the view. Yes, there was Tobias's place, prosperous and white-painted; she could just get a glimpse of the upper roofs and gables. It was always a sorrow and complaint that a low hill kept her from looking up at this farm from any of the windows, but now that she was at the farm itself she found herself regarding Tobias's home with a good deal of affection. She looked sharply with an apprehension of fire, but there was no whiff of alarming smoke against the dear sky.

"Now I must git me a drink o' that water first of anything," and she hastened to the creaking well-sweep and lowered the bucket. There was the same rusty, handleless tin dipper that she had left years before, standing on the shelf inside the well-curb. She was proud to find that the bucket was no heavier than ever, and was heartily thankful for the clear water. There never was such a well as that, and it seemed as if she had not been away a day. "What an old gal I be," said Mercy, with plaintive merriment. "Well, they ain't made no great changes since I was here last spring," and then she went over and held her face close against one of the kitchen windows, and took a hungry look at the familiar room. The bedroom door was open and a new sense of attachment to the place filled her heart. "It seems as if I was locked out o' my own home," she whispered as she looked in.

There were the same old spruce and pine boards that she had scrubbed so many times and trodden thin as she hurried to and fro about her work. It was very strange to see an unfamiliar chair or two, but the furnishings of a farm kitchen were much the same, and there

SARAH ORNE JEWETT

was no great change. Even the cradle was like that cradle in which her own children had been rocked. She gazed and gazed, poor old Mother Bascom, and forgot the present as her early life came back in vivid memories. At last she turned away from the window with a sigh.

The flowers that she had planted herself long ago had bloomed all summer in the garden; there were still some ragged sailors and the snowberries and phlox and her favorite white mallows, of which she picked herself a posy. "I'm glad the old place is so well took care of," she thought, gratefully. "An' they've new-silled the old barn I do declare, and battened the cracks to keep the dumb creatures warm. 'T was a sham-built barn anyways, but 't was the best I could do when the child'n needed something every handturn o' the day. It put me to some expense every year, tinkering of it up where the poor lumber warped and split. There, I enjoyed try'n to cope with things and gettin' the better of my disadvantages! The ground's too rich for me over there to Tobias's; I don't want things too easy, for my part. I feel most as young as ever I did, and I ain't agoin' to play helpless, not for nobody.

"I declare for 't, I mean to come up here by an' by a spell an' stop with the young folks, an' give 'em a good lift with their work. I ain't needed all the time to Tobias' s now, and they can hire help, while these can't. I've been favoring myself till I'm as soft as an old hoss that's right out of pasture an' can't pull two wheels without wheezin'."

There was a sense of companionship in the very weather. The bees were abroad as if it were summer, and a flock of little birds came fluttering down close to Mrs. Bascom as she sat on the doorstep. She remembered the biscuits in her pocket and ate them with a hunger she had seldom known of late, but she threw the crumbs generously to her feathered neighbors. The soft air, the brilliant or fading colors of the wide landscape, the comfortable feeling of relationship to her surroundings all served to put good old Mercy into a most peaceful state. There was only one thought that would not let her be quite happy. She could not get her sister-in-law Ruth Parlet out of her mind. And strangely enough the old grudge did not present itself with the usual power of aggravation; it was of their early friendship and Ruth's good fellowship that memories would come.

"I declare for 't, I wouldn't own up to the folks, but I should like to have a good visit with Ruth if so be that we could set aside the past," she said, resolutely at last. "I never thought I should come to it, but if she offered to make peace I wouldn't do nothin' to hinder it. Not to say but what I should have to free my mind on one or two points before we could start fair. I've waited forty year to make one remark to Ruthy Parlet. But there! we're gettin' to be old folks." Mercy rebuked herself gravely. "I don't want to go off with hard feelins' to nobody." Whether this was the culmination of a long, slow process of reconciliation, or whether Mrs. Bascom's placid satisfaction helped to hasten it by many stages, nobody could say. As she sat there she thought of many things; her life spread itself out like a picture; perhaps never before had she been able to detach herself from her immediate occupation in this way. She never had been aware of her own character and exploits to such a degree, and the minutes sped by as she thought with deep interest along the course of her own history. There was nothing she was ashamed of to an uncomfortable degree but the long animosity between herself and the children's aunt. How harsh she had been sometimes; she had even tried to prejudice everybody who listened to these tales of an offender. "I wa'n't more 'n half right, now I come to look myself full in the face," said Mercy Bascom, "and I never owned it till this day."

The sun was already past noon, and the good woman dutifully rose and with instant consciousness of resource glanced in at the kitchen window to tell the time by a familiar mark on the floor. "I needn't start just yet," she muttered. "Oh my! how I do wish I could git in and poke round into every corner! 'T would make this day just perfect."

"There now!" she continued, "p'raps they leave the key just where our folks used to." And in another minute the key lay in Mercy's worn old hand. She gave a shrewd look along the road, opened the door, which creaked what may have been a hearty welcome, and stood inside the dear old kitchen. She had not been in the house alone since she left it, but now she was nobody's guest. It was like some shell-fish finding its own old shell again and settling comfortably into the convolutions. Even we must not follow Mother Bascom about from the dark cellar to the hot little attic. She was not curious about the Browns' worldly goods; indeed, she was nearly unconscious of anything but the comfort of going up and down the short flight of stairs and looking out of her own windows with nobody to watch.

"There's the place where Tobias scratched the cupboard door with a nail. Didn't I thrash him for it good?" she said once with a proud remembrance of the time when she was a lawgiver and proprietor and he dependent.

At length a creeping fear stole over her lest the family might return. She stopped one moment to look back into the little bedroom. "How good I did use to sleep here," she said. "I worked as stout as I could the day through, and there wa'n't no wakin' up by two o'clock in the morning, and smellin' for fire and harkin' for thieves like I have to nowadays."

Mercy stepped away down the long sloping field like a young woman. It was a long walk back to Tobias's, even if one followed the pleasant footpaths across country. She was heavy-footed, but entirely light-hearted when she came safely in at the gate of the Bassett place. "I've done extra for me," she said as she put away her old shawl and bonnet; "but I'm goin' to git the best supper Tobias's folks have eat for a year," and so she did.

"I've be'n over to the old place to-day," she announced bravely to her son, who had finished his work and his supper and was now tipped back in his wooden arm-chair against the wall.

"You ain't, mother!" responded Tobias, with instant excitement. "Next fall, then, I won't take no for an answer but what you'll go to the fair and see what's goin'. You ain't footed it way over there?"

Mother Bascom nodded. "I have," she answered solemnly, a minute later, as if the nod were not enough.

"T'bias, son," she added, lowering her voice, "I ain't one to give in my rights, but I was thinkin' it all over about y'r Aunt Ruth Parlet"—

"Now if that ain't curi's!" exclaimed Tobias, bringing his chair down hastily upon all four legs. "I didn't know just how you'd take it, mother, but I see Aunt Ruth to-day to the fair, and she made everything o' me and wanted to know how you was, and she got me off from the rest, an' says she: 'I declare I should like to see your marm again. I wonder if she won't agree to let bygones be bygones.'"

"My sakes!" said Mercy, who was startled by this news. "'T is the hand o' Providence! How did she look, son?"

"A sight older 'n you look, but kind of natural too. One o' her sons' wives that she's made her home with, has led her a dance, folks say."

"Poor old creatur'! we'll have her over here, if your folks don't find fault. I've had her in my mind"—

Tobias's folks, in the shape of his wife and little Johnny, appeared from the outer kitchen. "I haven't had such a supper I don't know when," repeated the younger woman for at least the fifth time. "You must have been keepin' busy all day, Mother Bascom."

But Mother Bascom and Tobias looked at each other and laughed.

"I ain't had such a good time I don't know when, but my feet are all of a fidget now, and I've got to git to bed. I've be'n runnin' away since you've be'n gone, Ann!" said the pleased old soul, and then went away, still laughing, to her own room. She was strangely excited and satisfied, as if she had at last paid a long-standing debt. She could trudge across pastures as well as anybody, and the old grudge was done with. Mercy hardly noticed how her fingers trembled as she unhooked the old gray gown. The odor of sweet fern shook out fresh and strong as she smoothed and laid it carefully over a chair. There was a little rent in the skirt, but she could mend it by daylight.

The great harvest moon was shining high in the sky, and she needed no other light in the bedroom. "I've be'n a smart woman to work in my day, and I've airnt a little pleasurin'," said Mother Bascom sleepily to herself. "Poor Ruthy! so she looks old, does she? I'm goin' to tell her right out, 't was I that spoke first to Tobias."

GOING TO SHREWSBURY

The train stopped at a way station with apparent unwillingness, and there was barely time for one elderly passenger to be hurried on board before a sudden jerk threw her almost off her unsteady old feet and we moved on. At my first glance I saw only a perturbed old countrywoman, laden with a large basket and a heavy bundle tied up in an old-fashioned bundle-handkerchief; then I discovered that she was a friend of mine, Mrs. Peet, who lived on a small farm, several miles from the village. She used to be renowned for good butter and fresh eggs and the earliest cowslip greens; in fact, she always made the most of her farm's slender resources; but it was some time since I had seen her drive by from market in her ancient thorough-braced wagon.

The brakeman followed her into the crowded car, also carrying a number of packages. I leaned forward and asked Mrs. Peet to sit by me; it was a great pleasure to see her again. The brakeman seemed relieved, and smiled as he tried to put part of his burden into the rack overhead; but even the flowered carpet-bag was much too large, and he explained that he would take care of everything at the end of the car. Mrs. Peet was not large herself, but with the big basket, and the bundle-handkerchief, and some possessions of my own we had very little spare room.

"So this 'ere is what you call ridin' in the cars! Well, I do declare!" said my friend, as soon as she had recovered herself a little. She looked pale and as if she had been in tears, but there was the familiar gleam of good humor in her tired old eyes.

"Where in the world are you going, Mrs. Peet?" I asked.

"Can't be you ain't heared about me, dear?" said she. "Well, the world's bigger than I used to think 't was. I've broke up,—'t was the only thing to do,—and I'm a-movin' to Shrewsbury."

"To Shrewsbury? Have you sold the farm?" I exclaimed, with sorrow and surprise. Mrs. Peet was too old and too characteristic to be suddenly transplanted from her native soil, "'T wa'n't mine, the place wa'n't." Her pleasant face hardened slightly. "He was coaxed an' over-persuaded into signin' off before he was taken away. Is'iah, son of his sister that married old Josh Peet, come it over him about his bein' past work and how he'd do for him like an own son, an' we owed him a little somethin'. I'd paid off everythin' but that, an' was fool enough to leave it till the last, on account o' Is'iah's bein' a relation and not needin' his pay much as some others did. It's hurt me to have the place fall into other hands. Some wanted me to go right to law; but 't wouldn't be no use. Is'iah's smarter 'n I be about them matters. You see he's got my name on the paper, too;

he said 't was somethin' 'bout bein' responsible for the taxes. We was scant o' money, an' I was wore out with watchin' an' being broke o' my rest. After my tryin' hard for risin' forty-five year to provide for bein' past work, here I be, dear, here I be! I used to drive things smart, you remember. But we was fools enough in '72 to put about everythin' we had safe in the bank into that spool factory that come to nothin'. But I tell ye I could ha' kept myself long's I lived, if I could ha' held the place. I'd parted with most o' the woodland, if Is'iah 'd coveted it. He was welcome to that, 'cept what might keep me in oven-wood. I've always desired to travel an' see somethin' o' the world, but I've got the chance now when I don't value it no great."

"Shrewsbury is a busy, pleasant place," I ventured to say by way of comfort, though my heart was filled with rage at the trickery of Isaiah Peet, who had always looked like a fox and behaved like one.

"Shrewsbury's be'n held up consid'able for me to smile at," said the poor old soul, "but I tell ye, dear, it's hard to go an' live twenty-two miles from where you've always had your home and friends. It may divert me, but it won't be home. You might as well set out one o' my old apple-trees on the beach, so 't could see the waves come in,—there wouldn't be no please to it."

"Where are you going to live in Shrewsbury?" I asked presently.

"I don't expect to stop long, dear creatur'. I'm 'most seventy-six year old," and Mrs. Peet turned to look at me with pathetic amusement in her honest wrinkled face. "I said right out to Is'iah, before a roomful o' the neighbors, that I expected it of him to git me home an' bury me when my time come, and do it respectable; but I wanted to airn my livin', if 't was so I could, till then. He'd made sly talk, you see, about my electin' to leave the farm and go 'long some o' my own folks; but"—and she whispered this carefully—"he didn't give me no chance to stay there without hurtin' my pride and dependin' on him. I ain't said that to many folks, but all must have suspected. A good sight on 'em's had money of Is'iah, though, and they don't like to do nothin' but take his part an' be pretty soft spoken, fear it'll git to his ears. Well, well, dear, we'll let it be bygones, and not think of it no more;" but I saw the great tears roll slowly down her cheeks, and she pulled her bonnet forward impatiently, and looked the other way.

"There looks to be plenty o' good farmin' land in this part o' the country," she said, a minute later. "Where be we now? See them handsome farm buildings; he must be a well-off man." But I had to tell my companion that we were still within the borders of the old town where we had both been born. Mrs. Peet gave a pleased little laugh, like a girl. "I'm expectin' Shrewsbury to pop up any minute. I'm feared to be kerried right by. I wa'n't never aboard of the cars before, but I've so often thought about em' I don't know but it seems natural. Ain't it jest like flyin' through the air? I can't catch holt to see nothin'. Land! and here's my old cat goin' too, and never mistrustin'. I ain't told you that I'd fetched her."

"Is she in that basket?" I inquired with interest.

"Yis, dear. Truth was, I calculated to have her put out o' the misery o' movin', an spoke to one o' the Barnes boys, an' he promised me all fair; but he wa'n't there in season, an' I kind o' made excuse to myself to fetch her along. She's an' old creatur', like me, an' I can make shift to keep her some way or 'nuther; there's probably mice where we're goin', an' she's a proper mouser that can about keep herself if there's any sort o' chance. 'T will be somethin' o' home to see her goin' an' comin', but I expect we're both on us goin' to miss our old haunts. I'd love to know what kind o' mousin' there's goin' to be for me."

"You mustn't worry," I answered, with all the bravery and assurance that I could muster. "Your niece will be thankful to have you with her. Is she one of Mrs. Winn's daughters?"

"Oh, no, they ain't able; it's Sister Wayland's darter Isabella, that married the overseer of the gre't carriage-shop. I ain't seen her since just after she was married; but I turned to her first because I knew she was best able to have me, and then I can see just how the other girls is situated and make me some kind of a plot. I wrote to Isabella, though she *is* ambitious, and said 't was so I'd got to ask to come an' make her a visit, an' she wrote back she would be glad to have me; but she didn't write right off, and her letter was scented up dreadful strong with some sort o' essence, and I don't feel heartened about no great of a welcome. But there, I've got eyes, an' I can see *how*'t is when I git *where*'t is. Sister Winn's gals ain't married, an' they've always boarded, an' worked in the shop on trimmin's. Isabella' s well off; she had some means from her father's sister. I thought it all over by night an' day, an' I recalled that our folks kept Sister Wayland's folks all one winter, when he'd failed up and got into trouble. I'm reckonin' on sendin' over to-night an' gittin' the Winn gals to come and see me and advise. Perhaps some on 'em may know of somebody that'll take me for what help I can give about house, or some clever folks that have been lookin' for a smart cat, any ways; no, I don't know's I could let her go to strangers."

"There was two or three o' the folks round home that acted real warm-hearted towards me, an' urged me to come an' winter with 'em," continued the exile; "an' this mornin' I wished I'd agreed to, 't was so hard to break away. But now it's done I feel more 'n ever it's best. I couldn't bear to live right in sight o' the old place, and come spring I shouldn't 'prove of nothing Is'iah ondertakes to do with the land. Oh, dear sakes! now it comes hard with me not to have had no child'n. When I was young an' workin' hard and into everything, I felt kind of free an' superior to them that was so blessed, an' their houses cluttered up from mornin' till night, but I tell ye it comes home to me now. I'd be most willin' to own to even Is'iah, mean's he is; but I tell ye I'd took it out of him 'fore he was a grown man, if there 'd be'n any virtue in cow-hidin' of him. Folks don't look like wild creator's for nothin'. Is'iah's got fox blood in him, an' p'r'haps 't is his misfortune. His own mother always favored the looks of an old fox, true's the world; she was a poor tool,—a poor tool! I d' know's we ought to blame him same's we do.

"I've always been a master proud woman, if I was riz among the pastures," Mrs. Peet added, half to herself. There was no use in saying much to her; she was conscious of little beside her own thoughts and the smouldering excitement caused by this great crisis in her simple existence. Yet the atmosphere of her loneliness, uncertainty, and sorrow was so touching that after scolding again at her nephew's treachery, and finding the tears come fast to my eyes as she talked, I looked intently out of the car window, and tried to think what could be done for the poor soul. She was one of the old-time people, and I hated to have her go away; but even if she could keep her home she would soon be too feeble to live there alone, and some definite plan must be made for her comfort. Farms in that neighborhood were not valuable. Perhaps through the agency of the law and quite in secret, Isaiah Peet could be forced to give up his unrighteous claim. Perhaps, too, the Winn girls, who were really no longer young, might have saved something, and would come home again. But it was easy to make such pictures in one's mind, and I must do what I could through other people, for I was just leaving home for a long time. I wondered sadly about Mrs. Peet's future, and the ambitious Isabella, and the favorite Sister Winn's daughters, to whom, with all their kindliness of heart, the care of so old and perhaps so dependent an aunt might seem impossible. The truth about life in Shrewsbury would soon be known; more than half the short journey was already past.

To my great pleasure, my fellow-traveler now began to forget her own troubles in looking about her. She was an alert, quickly interested old soul, and this was a bit of neutral ground between the farm and Shrewsbury, where she was unattached and irresponsible. She had lived through the last tragic moments of her old life, and felt a certain relief, and Shrewsbury might be as far away as the other side of the Rocky Mountains for all the consciousness she had of its real existence. She was simply a traveler for the time being, and began to comment, with delicious phrases and shrewd understanding of human nature, on two or three persons near us who attracted her attention.

"Where do you s'pose they be all goin'?" she asked contemptuously. "There ain't none on 'em but what looks kind o' respectable. I'll warrant they've left work to home they'd ought to be doin'. I knowed, if ever I stopped to think, that cars was hived full o' folks, an' wa'n't run to an' fro for nothin'; but these can't be quite up to the average, be they? Some on 'em's real thrif'less? guess they've be'n shoved out o' the last place, an' goin' to try the next one,—*like me*, I suppose you'll want to say! Jest see that flauntin' old creatur' that looks like a stopped clock. There! everybody can't be o' one goodness, even preachers."

I was glad to have Mrs. Peet amused, and we were as cheerful as we could be for a few minutes. She said earnestly that she hoped to be forgiven for such talk, but there were some kinds of folks in the cars that she never had seen before. But when the conductor came to take her ticket she relapsed into her first state of mind, and was at a loss.

"You'll have to look after me, dear, when we get to Shrewsbury," she said, after we had spent some distracted moments in hunting for the ticket, and the cat had almost escaped from the basket, and the bundle-handkerchief had become untied and all its miscellaneous contents scattered about our laps and the floor. It was a touching collection of the last odds and ends of Mrs. Peet's housekeeping: some battered books, and singed holders for flatirons, and the faded little shoulder shawl that I had seen her wear many a day about her bent shoulders. There were her old tin match-box spilling all its matches, and a goose-wing for brushing up ashes, and her much-thumbed Leavitt's Almanac. It was most pathetic to see these poor trifles out of their places. At last the ticket was found in her left-hand woolen glove, where her stiff, work-worn hand had grown used to the feeling of it.

"I shouldn't wonder, now, if I come to like living over to Shrewsbury first-rate," she insisted, turning to me with a hopeful, eager look to see if I differed. "You see 't won't be so tough for me as if I hadn't always felt it lurking within me to go off some day or 'nother an' see how other folks did things. I do' know but what the Winn gals have laid up somethin' sufficient for us to take a house, with the little mite I've got by me. I might keep house for us all, 'stead o' boardin' round in other folks' houses. That I ain't never been demeaned to, but I dare say I should find it pleasant in some ways. Town folks has got the upper hand o' country folks, but with all their work an' pride they can't make a dandelion. I do' know the times when I've set out to wash Monday mornin's, an' tied out the line betwixt the old pucker-pear tree and the corner o' the barn, an' thought, 'Here I be with the same kind o' week's work right over again.' I'd wonder kind o' f'erce if I couldn't git out of it noways; an' now here I be out of it, and an uprooteder creatur' never stood on the airth. Just as I got to feel I had somethin' ahead come that spool-factory business. There! you know he never was a forehanded man; his health was slim, and he got discouraged pretty nigh before ever he begun. I hope he don't know I'm turned out o' the old place. 'Is'iah's well off; he'll do the right thing by ye,' says he. But my! I turned hot all over when I found out what I'd put my name to,—me that had always be'n counted a smart woman! I did undertake to read it over, but I couldn't sense it. I've told all the folks so when they laid it off on to me some: but hand-writin' is awful tedious readin' and my head felt that day as if the works was gone."

"I ain't goin' to sag on to nobody," she assured me eagerly, as the train rushed along. "I've got more work in me now than folks expects at my age. I may be consid'able use to Isabella. She's got a family, an' I'll take right holt in the kitchen or with the little gals. She had four on 'em, last I heared. Isabella was never one that liked house-work. Little gals! I do' know now but what they must be about grown, time doos slip away so. I expect I shall look outlandish to 'em. But there! everybody knows me to home, an' nobody knows me to Shrewsbury; 't won't make a mite o' difference, if I take holt willin'.'"

I hoped, as I looked at Mrs. Peet, that she would never be persuaded to cast off the gathered brown silk bonnet and the plain shawl that she had worn so many years; but Isabella might think it best to insist upon more modern fashions. Mrs. Peet suggested, as if it were a matter of little consequence, that she had kept it in mind to buy some mourning; but there were other things to be thought of first, and so she had let it go until winter, any way, or until she should be fairly settled in Shrewsbury.

"Are your nieces expecting you by this train?" I was moved to ask, though with all the good soul's ready talk and appealing manner I could hardly believe that she was going to Shrewsbury for more than a visit; it seemed as if she must return to the worn old farmhouse over by the sheep-lands. She answered that one of the Barnes boys had written a letter for her the day before, and there was evidently little uneasiness about her first reception.

We drew near the junction where I must leave her within a mile of the town. The cat was clawing indignantly at the basket, and her mistress grew as impatient of the car. She began to look very old and pale, my poor fellow-traveler, and said that she felt dizzy, going so fast. Presently the friendly red-cheeked young brakeman came along, bringing the carpet-bag and other possessions, and insisted upon taking the alarmed cat beside, in spite of an aggressive paw that had worked its way through the wicker prison. Mrs. Peet watched her goods disappear with suspicious eyes, and clutched her bundle-handkerchief as if it might be all that she could save. Then she anxiously got to her feet, much too soon, and when I said good-by to her at the car door she was ready to cry. I pointed to the car which she was to take next on the branch line of railway, and I assured her that it was only a few minutes' ride to Shrewsbury, and that I felt certain she would find somebody waiting. The sight of that worn, thin figure adventuring alone across the platform gave my heart a sharp pang as the train carried me away.

Some of the passengers who sat near asked me about my old friend with great sympathy, after she had gone. There was a look of tragedy about her, and indeed it had been impossible not to get a good deal of her history, as she talked straight on in the same tone, when we stopped at a station, as if the train were going at full speed, and some of her remarks caused pity and amusements by turns. At the last minute she said, with deep self-reproach, "Why, I haven't asked a word about your folks; but you'd ought to excuse such an old stray hen as I be."

In the spring I was driving by on what the old people of my native town call the sheep-lands road, and the sight of Mrs. Peet's former home brought our former journey freshly to my mind. I had last heard from her just after she got to Shrewsbury, when she had sent me a message.

"Have you ever heard how she got on?" I eagerly asked my companion.

"Didn't I tell you that I met her in Shrewsbury High Street one day?" I was answered. "She seemed perfectly delighted with everything. Her nieces have laid up a good bit of money, and are soon to leave the mill, and most thankful to have old Mrs. Peet with them. Somebody told me that they wished to buy the farm here, and come back to live, but she wouldn't hear of it, and thought they would miss too many privileges. She has been going to concerts and lectures this winter, and insists that Isaiah did her a good turn."

We both laughed. My own heart was filled with joy, for the uncertain, lonely face of this homeless old woman had often haunted me. The rain-blackened little house did certainly look dreary, and a whole lifetime of patient toil had left few traces. The pucker-pear tree was in full bloom, however, and gave a welcome gayety to the deserted door-yard.

A little way beyond we met Isaiah Peet, the prosperous money-lender, who had cheated the old woman of her own. I fancied that he looked somewhat ashamed, as he recognized us. To my surprise, he stopped his horse in most social fashion.

"Old Aunt Peet's passed away," he informed me briskly. "She had a shock, and went right off sudden yesterday forenoon. I'm about now tendin' to the funeral 'rangements. She's be'n extry smart, they say, all winter,—out to meetin' last Sabbath; never enjoyed herself so complete as she has this past month. She'd be'n a very hard-workin' woman. Her folks was glad to have her there, and give her every attention. The place here never was good for nothin'. The old gen'leman,—uncle, you know,—he wore hisself out tryin' to make a livin' off from it."

There was an ostentatious sympathy and half-suppressed excitement from bad news which were quite lost upon us, and we did not linger to hear much more. It seemed to me as if I had known Mrs. Peet better than any one else had known her. I had counted upon seeing her again, and hearing her own account of Shrewsbury life, its pleasures and its limitations. I wondered what had become of the cat and the contents of the faded bundle-handkerchief.

THE TAKING OF CAPTAIN BALL

I

There was a natural disinclination to the cares of housekeeping in the mind of Captain Ball, and he would have left the sea much earlier in life if he had not liked much better to live on board ship. A man was his own master there, and meddlesome neighbors and parsons and tearful women-folks could be made to keep their distance. But as years went on, and the extremes of weather produced much affliction in the shape of rheumatism, this, and the decline of the merchant service, and the degeneracy of common seamen, forced Captain Ball to come ashore for good. He regretted that he could no longer follow the sea, and, in spite of many alleviations, grumbled at his hard fate. He might have been condemned to an inland town, but in reality his house was within sight of tide-water, and he found plenty of companionship in the decayed seaport where he had been born and bred. There were several retired shipmasters who closely approached his own rank and dignity. They all gave other excuses than that of old age and infirmity for being out of business, took a sober satisfaction in their eleven o'clock bitters, and discussed the shipping list of the morning paper with far more interest than the political or general news of the other columns.

While Captain Asaph Ball was away on his long voyages he had left his house in charge of an elder sister, who was joint owner. She was a grim old person, very stern in matters of sectarian opinion, and the captain recognized in his heart of hearts that she alone was his superior officer. He endeavored to placate her with generous offerings of tea and camel's-hair scarfs and East Indian sweetmeats, not to speak of unnecessary and sometimes very beautiful china for the parties that she never gave, and handsome dress patterns with which she scorned to decorate her sinful shape of clay. She pinched herself to the verge of want in order to send large sums of money to the missionaries, but she saved the captain's money for him against the time when his willful lavishness and improvidence might find him a poor man. She was always looking forward to the days when he would be aged and forlorn, that burly seafaring brother of hers. She loved to remind him of his latter end, and in writing her long letters that were to reach him in foreign ports, she told little of the neighborhood news and results of voyages, but bewailed, in page after page, his sad condition of impenitence and the shortness of time. The captain would rather have faced a mutinous crew any day than his sister's solemn statements of this sort, but he loyally read them through with heavy sighs, and worked himself into his best broadcloth suit, at least once while he lay in port, to go to church on Sunday, out of good New England habit and respect to her opinions. It was not his sister's principles but her phrases that the captain failed to comprehend. Sometimes when he returned to his ship he took pains to write a letter to dear sister Ann, and to casually mention the fact of his attendance upon public worship, and even to recall the text and purport of the sermon. He was apt to fall asleep in his humble place at the very back of the church, and his report of the services would have puzzled a far less keen theologian than Miss Ann Ball. In fact these poor makeshifts of religious interest did not deceive her, and the captain had an uneasy consciousness that, to use his own expression, the thicker he laid on the words, the quicker she saw through them. And somehow or other that manly straightforwardness and honesty of his, that free-handed generosity, that true unselfishness which made him stick by his ship when the crew had run away from a poor black cook who was taken down with the yellow-fever, which made him nurse the frightened beggar as tenderly as a woman, and bring him back to life, and send him packing afterward with plenty of money in his pocket—all these fine traits that made Captain Ball respected in every port where his loud voice and clumsy figure and bronzed face were known, seemed to count for nothing with the stern sister. At least her younger brother thought so. But when, a few years after he came ashore for good, she died and left him alone in the neat old white house, which his instinctive good taste and his father's before him had made a museum of East Indian treasures, he found all his letters stored away with loving care after they had been read and reread into tatters, and among her papers such touching expressions of love and pride and longing for his soul's good, that poor Captain Asaph broke down altogether and cried like a school-boy. She had saved every line of newspaper which even mentioned his ships' names. She had loved him deeply in the repressed New England fashion, that under a gray and forbidding crust of manner, like a chilled lava bed, hides glowing fires of loyalty and devotion.

Sister Ann was a princess among housekeepers, and for some time after her death the captain was a piteous mourner indeed. No growing school-boy could be more shy and miserable in the presence of women than he, though nobody had a readier friendliness or more off-hand sailor ways among men. The few intimate family friends who came to his assistance at the time of his sister's illness and death added untold misery to the gloomy situation. Yet he received the minister with outspoken gratitude in spite of that worthy man's trepidation. Everybody said that poor Captain Ball looked as if his heart was broken. "I tell ye I feel as if I was tied in a bag of fleas," said the distressed mariner, and his pastor turned away to cough, hoping to hide the smile that would come. "Widders an' old maids, they're busier than the divil in a gale o' wind," grumbled the captain. "Poor Ann, she was worth every one of 'em lashed together, and here you find me with a head-wind every way I try to steer." The minister was a man at any rate; his very presence was a protection.

Some wretched days went by while Captain Ball tried to keep his lonely house with the assistance of one Silas Jenkins, who had made several voyages with him as cook, but they soon proved that the best of sailors may make the worst of housekeepers. Life looked darker and darker, and when, one morning, Silas inadvertently overheated and warped the new cooking stove, which had been the pride of Miss Ball's heart, the breakfastless captain dismissed him in a fit of blind rage. The captain was first cross and then abject when he went hungry, and in this latter stage was ready to abase himself enough to recall Widow Sparks, his sister's lieutenant, who lived close by in Ropewalk Lane, forgetting that he had driven her into calling him an old hog two days after the funeral. He groaned aloud as he thought of her, but reached for his hat and cane, when there came a gentle feminine rap at the door.

"Let 'em knock!" grumbled the captain, angrily, but after a moment's reflection, he scowled and went and lifted the latch.

There stood upon the doorstep a middle-aged woman, with a pleasant though determined face. The captain scowled again, but involuntarily opened his fore-door a little wider.

"Capt'in Asaph Ball, I presume?"

"The same," answered the captain.

"I've been told, sir, that you need a housekeeper, owing to recent affliction."

There was a squally moment of resistance in the old sailor's breast, but circumstances seemed to be wrecking him on a lee shore. Down came his flag on the run.

"I can't say but what I do, ma'am," and with lofty courtesy, such as an admiral should use to his foe of equal rank, the master of the house signified that his guest might enter. When they were seated opposite each other in the desolate sitting-room he felt himself the weaker human being of the two. Five years earlier, and he would have put to sea before the week's end, if only to gain the poor freedom of a coastwise lime schooner.

"Well, speak up, can't ye?" he said, trying to laugh. "Tell me what's the tax, and how much you can take hold and do, without coming to me for orders every hand's turn o' the day. I've had Silas Jinkins here, one o' my old ship's cooks; he served well at sea, and I thought he had some head; but we've been beat, I tell ye, and you'll find some work to put things ship-shape. He's gitting in years, that's the trouble; I oughtn't to have called on him," said Captain Ball, anxious to maintain even so poorly the dignity of his sex.

"I like your looks; you seem a good steady hand, with no nonsense about ye." He cast a shy glance at his companion, and would not have believed that any woman could have come to the house a stranger, and have given him such an immediate feeling of confidence and relief.

"I'll tell ye what's about the worst of the matter," and the captain pulled a letter out of his deep coat pocket. His feelings had been pent up too long. At the sight of the pretty handwriting and aggravatingly soft-spoken sentences, Asaph Ball was forced to inconsiderate speech. The would-be housekeeper pushed back her rocking-chair as he began, and tucked her feet under, beside settling her bonnet a little, as if she were close-reefed and anchored to ride out the gale.

"I'm in most need of an able person," he roared, "on account of this letter's settin' me adrift about knowing what to do. 'T is from a gal that wants to come and make her home here. Land sakes alive, puts herself right forrard! I don't want her, *an' I won't have her*. She may be a great-niece; I don't say she ain't; but what should I do with one o' them jiggetin' gals about? In the name o' reason, why should I be set out o' my course? I'm left at the mercy o' you women-folks," and the captain got stiffly to his feet. "If you've had experience, an' think you can do for me, why, stop an' try, an' I'll be much obleeged to ye. You'll find me a good provider, and we'll let one another alone, and get along some way or 'nother."

The captain's voice fairly broke; he had been speaking as if to a brother man; he was tired out and perplexed. His sister Ann had saved him so many petty trials, and now she was gone. The poor man had watched her suffer and seen her die, and he was as tender-hearted and

SARAH ORNE JEWETT

as lonely as a child, however he might bluster. Even such infrequent matters as family letters had been left to his busy sister. It happened that they had inherited a feud with an elder half-brother's family in the West, though the captain was well aware of the existence of this forth-putting great-niece, who had been craftily named for Miss Ann Ball, and so gained a precarious hold on her affections; but to harbor one of the race was to consent to the whole. Captain Ball was not a man to bring down upon himself an army of interferers and plunderers, and he now threw down the poor girl's well-meant letter with an outrageous expression of his feelings. Then he felt a silly weakness, and hastened to wipe his eyes with his pocket-handkerchief.

"I've been beat, I tell ye," he said brokenly.

There was a look of apparent sympathy, mingled with victory, on the housekeeper's face. Perhaps she had known some other old sailor of the same make, for she rose and turned her face aside to look out of the window until the captain's long upper lip had time to draw itself straight and stern again. Plainly she was a woman of experience and discretion.

"I'll take my shawl and bunnit right off, sir," she said, in a considerate little voice. "I see a-plenty to do; there'll be time enough after I get you your dinner to see to havin' my trunk here; but it needn't stay a day longer than you give the word."

"That's clever," said the captain. "I'll step right down street and get us a good fish, an' you can fry it or make us a chowder, just which you see fit. It now wants a little of eleven"—and an air of pleased anticipation lighted his face—"I must be on my way."

"If it's all the same to you, I guess we don't want no company till we get to rights a little. You're kind of tired out, sir," said the housekeeper, feelingly. "By-and-by you can have the young girl come an' make you a visit, and either let her go or keep her, 'cordin' as seems fit. I may not turn out to suit."

"What may I call you, ma'am?" inquired Captain Ball. "Mis' French? Not one o' them Fleet Street Frenches?" (suspiciously). "Oh, come from Massachusetts way!" (with relief).

"I was stopping with some friends that had a letter from some o' the minister's folks here, and they told how bad off you was," said Mrs. French, modestly. "I was out of employment, an' I said to myself that I should feel real happy to go and do for that Captain Ball. He knows what he wants, and I know what I want, and no flummery."

"You know somethin' o' life, I do declare," and the captain fairly beamed. "I never was called a hard man at sea, but I like to give my orders, and have folks foller 'em. If it was women-folks that wrote, they may have set me forth more 'n ordinary. I had every widder and single woman in town here while Ann lay dead, and my natural feelin's were all worked up. I see 'em dressed up and smirkin' and settin' their nets to ketch me when I was in an extremity. I wouldn't give a kentle o' sp'iled fish for the whole on 'em. I ain't a marryin' man, there's once for all for ye," and the old sailor stepped toward the door with some temper.

"Ef you'll write to the young woman, sir, just to put off comin' for a couple or three weeks," suggested Mrs. French.

"*This afternoon, ma'am,*" said the captain, as if it were the ay, ay, sir, of an able seaman who sprang to his duty of reefing the main-topsail.

Captain Ball walked down to the fish shop with stately steps and measured taps of his heavy cane. He stopped on the way, a little belated, and assured two or three retired ship-masters that he had manned the old brig complete at last; he even gave a handsome wink of his left eye over the edge of a glass, and pronounced his morning grog to be A No. 1, prime.

Mrs. French picked up her gown at each side with thumb and finger, and swept the captain a low courtesy behind his back as he went away; then she turned up the aforesaid gown and sought for one of the lamented Miss Ann Ball's calico aprons, and if ever a New England woman did a morning's work in an hour, it was this same Mrs. French.

"'T ain't every one knows how to make what I call a chowder," said the captain, pleased and replete, as he leaned back in his chair after dinner. "Mis' French, you shall have everything to do with, an' I ain't no kitchen colonel myself to bother ye."

There was a new subject for gossip in that seaport town. More than one woman had felt herself to be a fitting helpmate for the captain, and was confident that if time had been allowed, she could have made sure of even such wary game as he. When a stranger stepped in and occupied the ground at once, it gave nobody a fair chance, and Mrs. French was recognized as a presuming adventuress by all disappointed aspirants for the captain's hand. The captain was afraid at times that Mrs. French carried almost too many guns, but she made him so comfortable that she kept the upper hand, and at last he was conscious of little objection to whatever this able housekeeper proposed. Her only intimate friends were the minister and his wife, and the captain himself was so won over to familiarity by the kindness of his pastor in the time of affliction, that when after some weeks Mrs. French invited the good people to tea, Captain Ball sat manfully at the foot of his table, and listened with no small pleasure to the delighted exclamations of the parson's wife over his store of china and glass. There was a little feeling of guilt when he remembered how many times in his sister's day he had evaded such pleasant social occasions by complaint of inward malady, or by staying boldly among the wharves until long past supper-time, and forcing good Miss Ann to as many anxious excuses as if her brother's cranky ways were not as well known to the guests as to herself.

II

Mrs. Captain Topliff and Miss Miranda Hull were sitting together one late summer afternoon in Mrs. Topliff's south chamber. They were at work upon a black dress which was to be made over, and each sat by a front window with the blinds carefully set ajar.

"This is a real handy room to sew in," said Miranda, who had come early after dinner for a good long afternoon. "You git the light as long as there is any; and I do like a straw carpet; I don't feel's if I made so much work scatterin' pieces."

"Don't you have no concern about pieces," answered Mrs. Topliff, amiably. "I was precious glad to get you right on the sudden so. You see, I counted on my other dress lasting me till winter, and sort of put this by to do at a leisure time. I knew 't wa'n't fit to wear as 't was. Anyway, I've done dealin' with Stover; he told me, lookin' me right in the eye, that it was as good a wearin' piece o' goods as he had in the store. 'T was a real cheat; you can put your finger right through it."

"You've got some wear but of it," ventured Miranda, meekly, bending over her work. "I made it up quite a spell ago, I know. Six or seven years, ain't it, Mis' Topliff?"

"Yes, to be sure," replied Mrs. Topliff, with suppressed indignation; "but this we're to work on I had before the Centennial. I know I wouldn't take it to Philadelphy because 't was too good. An' the first two or three years of a dress don't count. You know how 't is; you just wear 'em to meetin' a pleasant Sunday, or to a funeral, p'r'aps, an' keep 'em in a safe cluset meanwhiles."

"Goods don't wear as 't used to," agreed Miranda; "but 't is all the better for my trade. Land! there's some dresses in this town I'm sick o' bein' called on to make good's new. Now I call you reasonable about such things, but there's some I could name"—Miss Hull at this point put several pins into her mouth, as if to guard a secret.

Mrs. Topliff looked up with interest. "I always thought Ann Ball was the meanest woman about such expense. She always looked respectable too, and I s'pose she 'd said the heathen was gittin' the good o' what she saved. She must have given away hundreds o' dollars in that direction."

"She left plenty too, and I s'pose Cap'n Asaph's Mis' French will get the good of it now," said Miranda through the pins. "Seems to me he's gittin' caught in spite of himself. Old vain creatur', he seemed to think all the women-folks in town was in love with him."

"Some was," answered Mrs. Topliff. "I think any woman that needed a home would naturally think 't was a good chance." She thought that Miranda had indulged high hopes, but wished to ignore them now.

"Some that had a home seemed inclined to bestow their affections, I observed," retorted the dressmaker, who had lost her little property by unfortunate investment, but would not be called homeless by Mrs. Topliff. Everybody knew that the widow had set herself down valiantly to besiege the enemy; but after this passage at arms between the friends they went on amiably with their conversation.

"Seems to me the minister and Mis' Calvinn are dreadful intimate at the Cap'n's. I wonder if the Cap'n's goin' to give as much to the heathen as his sister did?" said Mrs. Topliff, presently.

"I understood he told the minister that none o' the heathen was wuth it that ever he see," replied Miranda in a pinless voice at last. "Mr. Calvinn only laughed; he knows the Cap'n's ways. But I shouldn't thought Asaph Ball would have let his hired help set out and ask company to tea just four weeks from the day his only sister was laid away. 'T wa'n't feelin'."

"That Mis' French wanted to get the minister's folks to back her up, don't you understand?" was Mrs. Topliff's comment. "I should think the Calvinns wouldn't want to be so free and easy with a woman from nobody knows where. She runs in and out o' the parsonage any time o' day, as Ann Ball never took it upon her to do. Ann liked Mis' Calvinn, but she always had to go through with just so much, and be formal with everybody."

"I'll tell you something that exasperated *me*," confided the disappointed Miranda. "That night they was there to tea, Mis' Calvinn was praising up a handsome flowered china bowl that was on the table, with some new kind of a fancy jelly in it, and the Cap'n told her to take it along when she went home, if she wanted to, speakin' right out thoughtless, as men do; and that Mis' French chirped up, 'Yes, I'm glad; you ought to have somethin' to remember the cap'n's sister by,' says she. Can't you hear just how up an' comin' it was?"

"I can so," said Mrs. Topliff. "I see that bowl myself on Miss Calvinn's card-table, when I was makin' a call there day before yesterday. I wondered how she come by it. 'Tis an elegant bowl. Ann must have set the world by it, poor thing. Wonder if he ain't goin' to give remembrances to those that knew his sister ever since they can remember? Mirandy Hull, that Mis' French is a fox!"

"'T was Widow Sparks gave me the particulars," continued Mrs. Topliff. "She declared at first that never would she step foot inside his doors again, but I always thought the cap'n put up with a good deal. Her husband's havin' been killed in one o' his ships by a fall when he was full o' liquor, and her bein' there so much to help Ann, and their havin' provided for her all these years one way an' another, didn't give her the right to undertake the housekeepin' and direction o' everything soon as Ann died. She dressed up as if 't was for meetin', and 'tended the front door, and saw the folks that came. You'd thought she was ma'am of everything; and to hear her talk up to the cap'n! I thought I should die o' laughing when he blowed out at her. You know how he gives them great whoos when he's put about. 'Go below, can't ye, till your watch's called,' says he, same's 't was aboard ship; but there! everybody knew he was all broke down, and everything tried him. But to see her flounce out o' that back door!"

"'T was the evenin' after the funeral," Miranda said, presently. "I was there, too, you may rec'lect, seeing what I could do. The cap'n thought I was the proper one to look after her things, and guard against moths. He said there wa'n't no haste, but I knew better, an' told him I'd brought some camphire right with me. Well, did you git anything further out o' Mis' Sparks?"

"That French woman made all up with her, and Mis' Sparks swallowed her resentment. She's a good-feelin', ignorant kind o' woman, an' she needed the money bad," answered Mrs. Topliff. "If you'll never repeat, I'll tell you somethin' that'll make your eyes stick out, Miranda."

Miranda promised, and filled her mouth with pins preparatory to proper silence.

"You know the Balls had a half-brother that went off out West somewhere in New York State years ago. I don't remember him, but he brought up a family, and some of 'em came here an' made visits. Ann used to get letters from 'em sometimes, she's told me, and I dare say used to do for 'em. Well, Mis' Sparks says that there was a smart young Miss Ball, niece, or great-niece o' the cap'n, wrote on and wanted to come an' live with him for the sake o' the home—his own blood and kin, you see, and very needy—and Mis' Sparks heard 'em talk about her, and that wicked, low, offscourin' has got round Asaph Ball till he's consented to put the pore girl off. You see, she wants to contrive time to make him marry her, and then she'll do as she pleases about his folks. Now ain't it a shame? When I see her parade up the broad aisle, I want to stick out my tongue at her—I do so, right in meetin'. If the cap'n's goin' to have a shock within a year, I could wish it might be soon, to disappoint such a woman. Who is she, anyway? She makes me think o' some carr'on bird pouncin' down on us right out o' the air." Mrs. Topliff sniffed and jerked about in her chair, having worked herself into a fine fit of temper.

"There ain't no up nor down to this material, is there?" inquired Miranda, meekly. She was thinking that if she were as well off as Mrs. Topliff, and toward seventy years of age, she would never show a matrimonial disappointment in this open way. It was ridiculous for a woman who had any respect for herself and for the opinion of society. Miranda had much more dignity, and tried to cool off Mrs. Topliff's warmth by discussion of the black gown.

"'T ain't pleasant to have such a character among us. Do you think it is, Mirandy?" asked Mrs. Topliff, after a few minutes of silence. "She's a good-looking person, but with something sly about her. I don't mean to call on her again until she accounts for herself. Livin' nearer than any of Ann's friends, I thought there would be a good many ways I could oblige the cap'n if he'd grant the opportunity, but 't ain't so to be. Now Mr. Topliff was such an easy-goin', pleasant-tempered man, that I take time to remember others is made different."

Miranda smiled. Her companion had suffered many things from a most trying husband; it was difficult to see why she was willing to risk her peace of mind again.

"Cap'n Asaph looks now as meek as Moses," she suggested, as she pared a newly basted seam with her creaking scissors. "Mis' French, whoever she may be, has got him right under her thumb. I, for one, believe she'll never get him, for all her pains. He's as sharp as she is any day, when it comes to that; but he's made comfortable, and she starches his shirt bosoms so's you can hear 'em creak 'way across the meeting-house. I was in there the other night—she wanted to see me about some work—and 't was neat as wax, and an awful good scent o' somethin' they'd had for supper."

"That kind's always smart enough," granted the widow Topliff. "I want to know if she cooks him a hot supper every night? Well, she'll catch him if anybody can. Why don't you get a look into some o' the clusets, if you go there to work? Ann was so formal I never spoke up as I wanted to about seeing her things. They must have an awful sight of china, and as for the linen and so on that the cap'n and his father before him fetched home from sea, you couldn't find no end to it. Ann never made 'way with much. I hope the mice ain't hivin' into it and makin' their nests. Ann was very particular, but I dare say it wore her out tryin' to take care o' such a houseful."

"I'm going there Wednesday," said Miranda. "I'll spy round all I can, but I don't like to carry news from one house to another. I never was one to make trouble; 't would make my business more difficult than't is a'ready."

"I'd trust you," responded Mrs. Topliff, emphatically. "But there, Mirandy, you know you can trust me too, and anything you say goes no further."

"Yes'm," returned Miranda, somewhat absently. "To cut this the way you want it is going to give the folds a ter'ble skimpy look."

"I thought it would from the first," was Mrs. Topliff's obliging answer.

III

The captain could not believe that two months had passed since his sister's death, but Mrs. French assured him one evening that it was so. He had troubled himself very little about public opinion, though hints of his housekeeper's suspicious character and abominable intentions had reached his ears through more than one disinterested tale-bearer. Indeed, the minister and his wife were the only persons among the old family friends who kept up any sort of intercourse with Mrs. French. The ladies of the parish themselves had not dared to asperse her character to the gruff captain, but were contented with ignoring her existence and setting their husbands to the fray. "Why don't you tell him what folks think?" was a frequent question; but after a first venture even the most intimate and valiant friends were sure to mind their own business, as the indignant captain bade them. Two of them had been partially won over to Mrs. French's side by a taste of her good cooking. In fact, these were Captain Dunn and Captain Allister, who, at the eleven o'clock rendezvous, reported their wives as absent at the County Conference, and were promptly bidden to a chowder dinner by the independent Captain Ball, who gloried in the fact that neither of his companions would dare to ask a friend home unexpectedly. Our hero promised his guests that what they did not find in eatables they should make up in drinkables, and actually produced a glistening decanter of Madeira that had made several voyages in his father's ships while he himself was a boy. There were several casks and long rows of cobwebby bottles in the cellar, which had been provided against possible use in case of illness, but the captain rarely touched them, though he went regularly every morning for a social glass of what he frankly persisted in calling his grog. The dinner party proved to be a noble occasion, and Mrs. French won the esteem of the three elderly seamen by her discreet behavior, as well as by the flavor of the chowder.

They walked out into the old garden when the feast was over, and continued their somewhat excited discussion of the decline of shipping, on the seats of the ancient latticed summer-house. There Mrs. French surprised them by bringing out a tray of coffee, served in the handsome old cups which the captain's father had brought home from France. She was certainly a good-looking woman, and stepped modestly and soberly along the walk between the mallows and marigolds. Her feminine rivals insisted that she looked both bold and sly, but she minded her work like a steam-tug, as the captain whispered admiringly to his friends.

"Ain't never ascertained where she came from last, have ye?" inquired Captain Alister, emboldened by the best Madeira and the good-fellowship of the occasion.

"I'm acquainted with all I need to know," answered Captain Ball, shortly; but his face darkened, and when his guests finished their coffee they thought it was high time to go away.

Everybody was sorry that a jarring note had been struck on so delightful an occasion, but it could not be undone. On the whole, the dinner was an uncommon pleasure, and the host walked back into the house to compliment his housekeeper, though the sting of his friend's untimely question expressed itself by a remark that they had made most too much of an every-day matter by having the coffee in those best cups.

Mrs. French laughed. "'T will give 'em something to talk about; 't was excellent good coffee, this last you got, anyway," and Captain Asaph walked away, restored to a pleased and cheerful frame of mind. When he waked up after a solid after-dinner nap, Mrs. French, in her decent afternoon gown, as calm as if there had been no company to dinner, was just coming down the front stairs.

She seated herself by the window, and pretended to look into the street. The captain shook his newspaper at an invading fly. It was early September and flies were cruelly persistent. Somehow his nap had not entirely refreshed him, and he watched his housekeeper with something like disapproval.

"I want to talk with you about something, sir," said Mrs. French.

"She's going to raise her pay," the captain grumbled to himself. "Well, speak out, can't ye ma'am?" he said.

"You know I've been sayin' all along that you ought to get your niece"—

"She's my *great*-niece," blew the captain, "an' I don't know as I want her." The awful certainty came upon him that those hints were well-founded about Mrs. French's determination to marry him, and his stormy nature rose in wild revolt. "Can't you keep your place, ma'am?" and he gave a great *whoo!* as if he were letting off superabundant steam. She might prove to carry too many guns for him, and he grew very red in the face. It was a much worse moment than when a vessel comes driving at you amidships out of the fog.

"Why, yes, sir, I should be glad to keep my place," said Mrs. French, taking the less grave meaning of his remark by instinct, if not by preference; "only it seems your duty to let your great-niece come some time or other, and I can go off. Perhaps it is an untimely season to speak, about it, but, you see, I have had it in mind, and now I've got through with the preserves, and there's a space between now and house-cleaning, I guess you'd better let the young woman come. Folks have got wind about your refusing her earlier, and think hard of me: my position isn't altogether pleasant," and she changed color a little, and looked him full in the face.

The captain's eyes fell. He did owe her something. He never had been so comfortable in his life, on shore, as she had made him. She had heard some cursed ill-natured speeches, and he very well knew that a more self-respecting woman never lived. But now her moment of self-assertion seemed to have come, and, to use his own words, she had him fast. Stop! there was a way of escape.

"Then I *will* send for the gal. Perhaps you're right, ma'am. I've slept myself into the doldrums. *Whoo! whoo!*" he said, loudly—anything to gain a little time. "Anything you say, ma'am," he protested. "I've got to step down-town on some business," and the captain fled with ponderous footsteps out through the dining-room to the little side entry where he hung his hat; then a moment later he went away, clicking his cane along the narrow sidewalk.

He had escaped that time, and wrote the brief note to his great-niece, Ann Ball—how familiar the name looked!—with a sense of victory. He dreaded the next interview with his housekeeper, but she was business-like and self-possessed, and seemed to be giving him plenty of time. Then the captain regretted his letter, and felt as if he were going to be broken up once more in his home comfort. He spoke only when it was absolutely necessary, and simply nodded his head when Mrs. French said that she was ready to start as soon as she showed the young woman about the house. But what favorite dishes were served the captain in those intervening days! and there was one cool evening beside, when the housekeeper had the social assistance of a fire in the Franklin stove. The captain thought that his only safety lay in sleep, and promptly took that means of saving himself from a dangerous conversation. He even went to a panorama on Friday night, a diversion that would usually be quite beneath his dignity. It was difficult to avoid asking Mrs. French to accompany him, she helped him on with his coat so pleasantly, but "she'd git her claws on me comin' home perhaps," mused the self-distrustful mariner, and stoutly went his way to the panorama alone. It was a very dull show indeed, and he bravely confessed it, and then was angry at a twinkle in Mrs. French's eyes. Yet he should miss the good creature, and for the life of him he could not think lightly of her. "She well knows how able she is to do for me. Women-folks is cap'ns ashore," sighed the captain as he went upstairs to bed.

"Women-folks is cap'ns ashore," he repeated, in solemn confidence to one of his intimate friends, as they stood next day on one of the deserted wharves, looking out across the empty harbor roads. There was nothing coming in. How they had watched the deep-laden ships enter between the outer capes and drop their great sails in home waters! How they had ruled those ships, and been the ablest ship-masters of their day, with nobody to question their decisions! There is no such absolute monarchy as a sea-captain's. He is a petty king, indeed, as he sails the high seas from port to port.

There was a fine easterly breeze and a bright sun that day, but Captain Ball came toiling up the cobble-stoned street toward his house as if he were vexed by a headwind. He carried a post-card between his thumb and finger, and grumbled aloud as he stumped along. "Mis' French!" he called, loudly, as he opened the door, and that worthy woman appeared with a floured apron, and a mind divided between her employer's special business and her own affairs of pie-making.

"She's coming this same day," roared the captain. "Might have given some notice, I'm sure. 'Be with you Saturday afternoon,' and signed her name. That's all she's written. Whoo! whoo! 'tis a dreadful close day," and the poor old fellow fumbled for his big silk handkerchief. "I don't know what train she'll take. I ain't going to hang round up at the depot; my rheumatism troubles me."

"I wouldn't, if I was you," answered Mrs. French, shortly, and turned from him with a pettish movement to open the oven door.

The captain passed into the sitting-room, and sat down heavily in his large chair. On the wall facing him was a picture of his old ship the Ocean Rover leaving the harbor of Bristol. It was not valuable as a marine painting, but the sea was blue in that picture, and the white canvas all spread to the very sky-scrapers; it was an emblem of that freedom which Captain Asaph Ball had once enjoyed. Dinner that day was a melancholy meal, and after it was cleared away the master of the house forlornly watched Mrs. French gather an armful of her own belongings, and mount the stairs as if she were going to pack her box that very afternoon. It did not seem possible that she meant to leave before Monday, but the captain could not bring himself to ask any questions. He was at the mercy of womankind. "A jiggeting girl. I don't know how to act with her. She sha'n't rule me," he muttered to himself. "She and Mis' French may think they've got things right to their hands, but I'll stand my ground—I'll stand my ground," and the captain gently slid into the calmer waters of his afternoon nap.

When he waked the house was still, and with sudden consciousness of approaching danger, and a fear lest Mrs. French might have some last words to say if she found him awake, he stole out of his house as softly as possible and went down-town, hiding his secret woes and joining in the long seafaring reminiscences with which he and his friends usually diverted themselves. As he came up the street again toward supper-time, he saw that the blinds were thrown open in the parlor windows, and his heart began to beat loudly. He could hear women's voices, and he went in by a side gate and sought the quiet garden. It had suffered from a touch of frost; so had the captain.

Mrs. French heard the gate creak, and presently she came to the garden door at the end of the front entry. "Come in, won't ye, cap'n?" she called, persuasively, and with a mighty sea oath the captain rose and obeyed.

The house was still. He strode along the entry lite a brave man: there was nothing of the coward about Asaph Ball when he made up his mind to a thing. There was nobody in the best parlor, and he turned toward the sitting-room, but there sat smiling Mrs. French.

"Where is the gal?" blew the captain.

"Here I be, sir," said Mrs. French, with a flushed and beaming face. "I thought 't was full time to put you out of your misery."

"What's all this mean? *Whoo! whoo!*"

"Here I be; take me or leave me, uncle," answered the housekeeper: she began to be anxious, the captain looked so bewildered and irate. "Folks seemed to think that you was peculiar, and I was impressed that it would be better to just come first without a word's bein' said, and find out how you an' me got on; then, if we didn't make out, nobody 'd be bound. I'm sure I didn't want to be."

"Who was that I heard talking with ye as I come by?" blew the captain very loud.

"That was Mis' Cap'n Topliff; an' an old cat she is," calmly replied Mrs. French. "She hasn't been near me before this three months, but plenty of stories she's set goin' about us, and plenty of spyin' she's done. I thought I'd tell you who I was within a week after I come, but I found out how things was goin', and I had to spite 'em well before I got through. I expected that something would turn up, an' the whole story get out. But we've been middlin' comfortable, haven't we, sir? an' I thought 't was 'bout time to give you a little surprise. Mis' Calvinn and the minister knows the whole story," she concluded: "I wouldn't have kep' it from them. Mis' Calvinn said all along 't would be a good lesson"—

"Who wrote that card from the post-office?" demanded the captain, apparently but half persuaded.

"I did," said Mrs. French.

"Good Hector, you women-folks!" but Captain Ball ventured to cross the room and establish himself in his chair. Then, being a man of humor, he saw that he had a round turn on those who had spitefufly sought to question him.

"You needn't let on, that you haven't known me all along," suggested Mrs. French. "I should be pleased if you would call me by my Christian name, sir. I was married to Mr. French only a short time; he was taken away very sudden. The letter that came after aunt's death was directed to my maiden name, but aunt knew all about me. I've got some means, an' I ain't distressed but what I can earn my living."

"They don't call me such an old Turk, I hope!" exclaimed the excited captain, deprecating the underrated estimate of himself which was suddenly presented. "I ain't a hard man at sea, now I tell ye," and he turned away, much moved at the injustice of society. "I've got no head for geneology. Ann usually set in to give me the family particulars when I was logy with sleep a Sunday night. I thought you was a French from Massachusetts way."

"I had to say somethin'," responded the housekeeper, promptly.

"Well, well!" and a suppressed laugh shook the captain like an earthquake. He was suddenly set free from his enemies, while an hour before he had been hemmed in on every side.

They had a cheerful supper, and Ann French cut a pie, and said, as she passed him more than a quarter part of it, that she thought she should give up when she was baking that morning, and saw the look on his face as he handed her the post-card.

SARAH ORNE JEWETT

"You're fit to be captain of a privateer," acknowledged Captain Asaph Ball, handsomely. The complications of shore life were very astonishing to this seafaring man of the old school.

Early on Monday morning he had a delightful sense of triumph. Captain Allister, who was the chief gossip of the waterside club, took it upon himself—a cheap thing to do, as everybody said afterwards—to ask many questions about those unvalued relatives of the Balls, who had settled long ago in New York State. Were there any children left of the captain's half-brother's family?

"I've got a niece living—a great-niece she is," answered Captain Ball, with a broad smile—"makes me feel old. You see, my half-brother was a grown man when I was born. I never saw him scarcely; there was some misunderstanding an' he always lived with his own mother's folks; and father, he married again, and had me and Ann thirty year after. Why, my half-brother 'd been 'most a hundred; I don't know but more."

Captain Ball spoke in a cheerful tone; the audience meditated, and Captain Allister mentioned meekly that time did slip away.

"Ever see any of 'em?" he inquired. In some way public interest was aroused in the niece.

"Ever see any of 'em?" repeated the captain, in a loud tone. "You fool, Allister, who's keepin' my house this minute? Why, Ann French; Ann Ball that was, and a smart, likely woman she is. I ain't a marryin' man: there's been plenty o' fools to try me. I've been picked over well by you and others, and I thought if 't pleased you, you could take your own time."

The honest captain for once lent himself to deception. One would have thought that he had planned the siege himself. He took his stick from where it leaned against a decaying piece of ship-timber and went clicking away. The explanation of his housekeeping arrangements was not long in flying about the town, and Mrs. Captain Topliff made an early call to say that she had always suspected it from the first, from the family likeness.

From this time Captain Ball submitted to the rule of Mrs. French, and under her sensible and fearless sway became, as everybody said, more like other people than ever before. As he grew older it was more and more convenient to have a superior officer to save him from petty responsibilities. But now and then, after the first relief at finding that Mrs. French was not seeking his hand in marriage, and that the jiggeting girl was a mere fabrication, Captain Ball was both surprised and a little ashamed to discover that something in his heart had suffered disappointment in the matter of the great-niece. Those who knew him well would have as soon expected to see a flower grow out of a cobblestone as that Captain Asaph Ball should hide such a sentiment in his honest breast. He had fancied her a pretty girl in a pink dress, who would make some life in the quiet house, and sit and sing at her sewing by the front window, in all her foolish furbelows, as he came up the street.

BY THE MORNING BOAT

On the coast of Maine, where many green islands and salt inlets fringe the deep-cut shore line; where balsam firs and bayberry bushes send their fragrance far seaward, and song-sparrows sing all day, and the tide runs plashing in and out among the weedy ledges; where cowbells tinkle on the hills and herons stand in the shady coves,—on the lonely coast of Maine stood a small gray house facing the morning light. All the weather-beaten houses of that region face the sea apprehensively, like the women who live in them.

This home of four people was as bleached and gray with wind and rain as one of the pasture rocks close by. There were some cinnamon rose bushes under the window at one side of the door, and a stunted lilac at the other side. It was so early in the cool morning that nobody was astir but some shy birds, that had come in the stillness of dawn to pick and flutter in the short grass.

They flew away together as some one softly opened the unlocked door and stepped out. This was a bent old man, who shaded his eyes with his hand, and looked at the west and the east and overhead, and then took a few lame and feeble steps farther out to see a wooden vane on the barn. Then he sat down on the doorstep, clasped his hands together between his knees, and looked steadily out to sea, scanning the horizon where some schooners had held on their course all night, with a light westerly breeze. He seemed to be satisfied at sight of the weather, as if he had been anxious, as he lay unassured in his north bedroom, vexed with the sleeplessness of age and excited by thoughts of the coming day. The old seaman dozed as he sat on the doorstep, while dawn came up and the world grew bright; and the little birds returned, fearfully at first, to finish their breakfast, and at last made bold to hop close to his feet.

After a time some one else came and stood in the open door behind him.

"Why, father! seems to me you've got an early start; 't ain't but four o'clock. I thought I was foolish to get up so soon, but 't wa'n't so I could sleep."

"No, darter." The old man smiled as he turned to look at her, wide awake on the instant. "'T ain't so soon as I git out some o' these 'arly mornin's. The birds wake me up singin', and it's plenty light, you know. I wanted to make sure 'Lisha would have a fair day to go."

"I expect he'd have to go if the weather wa'n't good," said the woman.

"Yes, yes, but 'tis useful to have fair weather, an' a good sign some says it is. This is a great event for the boy, ain't it?"

"I can't face the thought o' losin' on him, father." The woman came forward a step or two and sat down on the doorstep. She was a hard-worked, anxious creature, whose face had lost all look of youth. She was apt, in the general course of things, to hurry the old man and to spare little time for talking, and he was pleased by this acknowledged unity of their interests. He moved aside a little to give her more room, and glanced at her with a smile, as if to beg her to speak freely. They were both undemonstrative, taciturn New Englanders; their hearts were warm with pent-up feeling, that summer morning, yet it was easier to understand one another through silence than through speech.

"No, I couldn't git much sleep," repeated the daughter at last. "Some things I thought of that ain't come to mind before for years,—things I don't relish the feelin' of, all over again."

"'T was just such a mornin' as this, pore little 'Lisha's father went off on that last v'y'ge o' his," answered the old sailor, with instant comprehension. "Yes, you've had it master hard, pore gal, ain't you? I advised him against goin' off on that old vessel with a crew that wa'n't capable."

"Such a mornin' as this, when I come out at sun-up, I always seem to see her top-s'ils over there beyond the p'int, where she was to anchor. Well, I thank Heaven 'Lisha was averse to goin' to sea," declared the mother.

"There's dangers ashore, Lucy Ann," said the grandfather, solemnly; but there was no answer, and they sat there in silence until the old man grew drowsy again.

"Yisterday was the first time it fell onto my heart that 'Lisha was goin' off," the mother began again, after a time had passed. "P'r'aps folks was right about our needing of him. I've been workin' every way I could to further him and git him a real good chance up to Boston, and now that we've got to part with him I don't see how to put up with it."

"All nateral," insisted the old man. "My mother wept the night through before I was goin' to sail on my first v'y'ge; she was kind of satisfied, though, when I come home next summer, grown a full man, with my savin's in my pocket, an' I had a master pretty little figured shawl I'd bought for her to Bristol."

"I don't want no shawls. Partin' is partin' to me," said the woman.

"'T ain't everybody can stand in her fore-door an' see the chimbleys o' three child'n's houses without a glass," he tried eagerly to console her.

SARAH ORNE JEWETT

"All ready an' willin' to do their part for you, so as you could let 'Lisha go off and have his chance."

"I don't know how it is," she answered, "but none on 'em never give me the rooted home feelin' that 'Lisha has. They was more varyin' and kind o' fast growin' and scatterin'; but 'Lisha was always 'Lisha when he was a babe, and I settled on him for the one to keep with me."

"Then he's just the kind to send off, one you ain't got to worry about. They're all good child'n," said the man. "We've reason to be thankful none on 'em's been like some young sprigs, more grief 'n glory to their folks. An' I ain't regrettin' 'Lisha's goin' one mite; I believe you'd rather go on doin' for him an' cossetin'. I think 't was high time to shove him out o' the nest."

"You ain't his mother," said Lucy Ann.

"What be you goin' to give him for his breakfast?" asked the stern grandfather, in a softened, less business-like voice.

"I don't know's I'd thought about it, special, sir. I did lay aside that piece o' apple pie we had left yisterday from dinner," she confessed.

"Fry him out a nice little crisp piece o' pork, Lucy Ann, an' 't will relish with his baked potatoes. He'll think o' his breakfast more times 'n you expect. I know a lad's feelin's when home's put behind him."

The sun was up clear and bright over the broad sea inlet to the eastward, but the shining water struck the eye by its look of vacancy. It was broad daylight, and still so early that no sails came stealing out from the farmhouse landings, or even from the gray groups of battered fish-houses that overhung, here and there, a sheltered cove. Some crows and gulls were busy in the air; it was the time of day when the world belongs more to birds than to men.

"Poor 'Lisha!" the mother went on compassionately. "I expect it has been a long night to him. He seemed to take it in, as he was goin' to bed, how 't was his last night to home. I heard him thrashin' about kind o' restless, sometimes."

"Come, Lucy Ann, the boy ought to be stirrin'!" exclaimed the old sailor, without the least show of sympathy. "He's got to be ready when John Sykes comes, an' he ain't so quick as some lads."

The mother rose with a sigh, and went into the house. After her own sleepless night, she dreaded to face the regretful, sleepless eyes of her son; but as she opened the door of his little bedroom, there lay Elisha sound asleep and comfortable to behold. She stood watching him with gloomy tenderness until he stirred uneasily, his consciousness roused by the intentness of her thought, and the mysterious current that flowed from her wistful, eager eyes.

But when the lad waked, it was to a joyful sense of manliness and responsibility; for him the change of surroundings was coming through natural processes of growth, not through the uprooting which gave his mother such an aching heart.

A little later Elisha came out to the breakfast-table, arrayed in his best sandy-brown clothes set off with a bright blue satin cravat, which had been the pride and delight of pleasant Sundays and rare holidays. He already felt unrelated to the familiar scene of things, and was impatient to be gone. For one thing, it was strange to sit down to breakfast in Sunday splendor, while his mother and grandfather and little sister Lydia were in their humble every-day attire. They ate in silence and haste, as they always did, but with a new constraint and awkwardness that forbade their looking at one another. At last the head of the household broke the silence with simple straightforwardness.

"You've got an excellent good day, 'Lisha. I like to have a fair start myself. 'T ain't goin' to be too hot; the wind's working into the north a little."

"Yes, sir," responded Elisha.

"The great p'int about gittin' on in life is bein' able to cope with your headwinds," continued the old man earnestly, pushing away his plate. "Any fool can run before a fair breeze, but I tell ye a good seaman is one that gits the best out o' his disadvantages. You won't be treated so pretty as you expect in the store, and you'll git plenty o' blows to your pride; but you keep right ahead, and if you can't run before the wind you can always beat. I ain't no hand to preach, but preachin' ain't goin' to sarve ye now. We've gone an' fetched ye up the best we could, your mother an' me, an' you can't never say but you've started amongst honest folks. If a vessel's built out o' sound timber an' has got good lines for sailin', why then she's seaworthy; but if she ain't, she ain't; an' a mess o' preachin' ain't goin' to alter her over. Now you're standin' out to sea, my boy, an' you can bear your home in mind and work your way, same's plenty of others has done."

It was a solemn moment; the speaker's voice faltered, and little Lydia dried her tearful blue eyes with her gingham apron. Elisha hung his head, and patted the old spotted cat which came to rub herself against his trowsers-leg. The mother rose hastily, and hurried into the pantry close by. She was always an appealing figure, with her thin shoulders and faded calico gowns; it was difficult to believe that she had once been the prettiest girl in that neighborhood. But her son loved her in his sober, undemonstrative way, and was full of plans for coming home, rich and generous enough to make her proud and happy. He was half pleased and half annoyed because his leave-taking was of such deep concern to the household.

"Come, Lyddy, don't you take on," he said, with rough kindliness. "Let's go out, and I'll show you how to feed the pig and 'tend to the chickens. You'll have to be chief clerk when I'm gone."

They went out to the yard, hand in hand. Elisha stopped to stroke the old cat again, as she ran by his side and mewed. "I wish I was off and done with it; this morning does seem awful long," said the boy.

"Ain't you afraid you'll be homesick an' want to come back?" asked the little sister timidly; but Elisha scorned so poor a thought.

"You'll have to see if grandpa has 'tended to these things, the pig an' the chickens," he advised her gravely. "He forgets 'em sometimes when I'm away, but he would be cast down if you told him so, and you just keep an eye open, Lyddy. Mother's got enough to do inside the house. But grandsir'll keep her in kindlin's; he likes to set and chop in the shed rainy days, an' he'll do a sight more if you'll set with him, an' let him get goin' on his old seafarin' times."

Lydia nodded discreetly.

"An', Lyddy, don't you loiter comin' home from school, an' don't play out late, an' get 'em fussy, when it comes cold weather. And you tell Susy Draper,"—the boy's voice sounded unconcerned, but Lydia glanced at him quickly,—"you tell Susy Draper that I was awful sorry she was over to her aunt's, so I couldn't say good-by."

Lydia's heart was the heart of a woman, and she comprehended. Lydia nodded again, more sagely than before.

"See here," said the boy suddenly. "I'm goin' to let my old woodchuck out."

Lydia's face was blank with surprise. "I thought you promised to sell him to big Jim Hooper."

"I did, but I don't care for big Jim Hooper; you just tell him I let my wood-chuck go."

The brother and sister went to their favorite playground between the ledges, not far from the small old barn. Here was a clumsy box with wire gratings, behind which an untamed little wild beast sat up and chittered at his harmless foes. "He's a whopping old fellow," said Elisha admiringly. "Big Jim Hooper sha'n't have him!" and as he opened the trap, Lydia had hardly time to perch herself high on the ledge, before the woodchuck tumbled and scuttled along the short green turf, and was lost among the clumps of juniper and bayberry just beyond.

"I feel just like him," said the boy. "I want to get up to Boston just as bad as that. See here, now!" and he flung a gallant cart-wheel of himself in the same direction, and then stood on his head and waved his legs furiously in the air. "I feel just like that."

Lydia, who had been tearful all the morning, looked at him in vague dismay. Only a short time ago she had never been made to feel that her brother was so much older than herself. They had been constant playmates; but now he was like a grown man, and cared no longer for their old pleasures. There was all possible difference between them that there can be between fifteen years and twelve, and Lydia was nothing but a child.

"Come, come, where be ye?" shouted the old grandfather, and they both started guiltily. Elisha rubbed some dry grass out of his short-cropped hair, and the little sister came down from her ledge. At that moment the real pang of parting shot through her heart; her brother belonged irrevocably to a wider world.

"Ma'am Stover has sent for ye to come over; she wants to say good-by to ye!" shouted the grandfather, leaning on his two canes at the end of the barn. "Come, step lively, an' remember you ain't got none too much time, an' the boat ain't goin' to wait a minute for nobody."

"Ma'am Stover?" repeated the boy, with a frown. He and his sister knew only too well the pasture path between the two houses. Ma'am Stover was a bedridden woman, who had seen much trouble,—a town charge in her old age. Her neighbors gave to her generously out of their own slender stores. Yet with all this poverty and dependence, she held firm sway over the customs and opinions of her acquaintance, from the uneasy bed where she lay year in and year out, watching the far sea line beyond a pasture slope.

The young people walked fast, sometimes running a little way, light-footed, the boy going ahead, and burst into their neighbor's room out of breath.

She was calm and critical, and their excitement had a sudden chill.

"So the great day's come at last, 'Lisha?" she asked; at which 'Lisha was conscious of unnecessary aggravation.

"I don't know's it's much of a day—to anybody but me," he added, discovering a twinkle in her black eyes that was more sympathetic than usual. "I expected to stop an' see you last night; but I had to go round and see all our folks, and when I got back 't was late and the tide was down, an' I knew that grandsir couldn't git the boat up all alone to our lower landin'."

"Well, I didn't forgit you, but I thought p'r'aps you might forgit me, an' I'm goin' to give ye somethin'. 'T is for your folks' sake; I want ye to tell 'em so. I don't want ye never to part with it, even if it fails to work and you git proud an' want a new one. It's been a sight o' company to me." She reached up, with a flush on her wrinkled cheeks and tears in her eyes, and took a worn old silver watch from its nail, and handed it, with a last look at its white face and large gold hands, to the startled boy.

"Oh, I can't take it from ye, Ma'am Stover. I'm just as much obliged to you," he faltered.

"There, go now, dear, go right along." said the old woman, turning quickly away. "Be a good boy for your folks' sake. If so be that I'm here when you come home, you can let me see how well you've kep' it."

The boy and girl went softly out, leaving the door wide open, as Ma'am Stover liked to have it in summer weather, her windows being small and few. There were neighbors near enough to come and shut it, if a heavy shower blew up. Sometimes the song sparrows and whippoorwills came hopping in about the little bare room.

"I felt kind of 'shamed to carry off her watch," protested Elisha, with a radiant face that belied his honest words.

"Put it on," said proud little Lydia, trotting alongside; and he hooked the bright steel chain into his buttonhole, and looked down to see how it shone across his waistcoat. None of his friends had so fine a watch; even his grandfather's was so poor a timekeeper that it was rarely worn except as a decoration on Sundays or at a funeral. They hurried home. Ma'am Stover, lying in her bed, could see the two slight figures nearly all the way on the pasture path; flitting along in their joyful haste.

It was disappointing that the mother and grandfather had so little to say about the watch. In fact, Elisha's grandfather only said "Pore creatur'" once or twice, and turned away, rubbing his eyes with the back of his hand. If Ma'am Stover had chosen to give so rich a gift, to know the joy of such generosity, nobody had a right to protest. Yet nobody knew how much the poor wakeful soul would miss the only one of her meagre possessions that seemed alive and companionable in lonely hours. Somebody had said once that there were chairs that went about on wheels, made on purpose for crippled persons like Ma'am Stover; and Elisha's heart was instantly filled with delight at the remembrance. Perhaps before long, if he could save some money and get ahead, he would buy one of those chairs and send it down from Boston; and a new sense of power filled his honest heart. He had dreamed a great many dreams already of what he meant to do with all his money, when he came home rich and a person of consequence, in summer vacations.

The large leather valise was soon packed, and its owner carried it out to the roadside, and put his last winter's overcoat and a great new umbrella beside it, so as to be ready when John Sykes came with the wagon. He was more and more anxious to be gone, and felt no sense of his old identification with the home interests. His mother said sadly that he would be gone full soon enough, when he joined his grandfather in accusing Mr. Sykes of keeping them waiting forever and making him miss the boat. There were three rough roundabout miles to be traveled to the steamer landing, and the Sykes horses were known to be slow. But at last the team came nodding in sight over a steep hill in the road.

Then the moment of parting had come, the moment toward which all the long late winter and early summer had looked. The boy was leaving his plain little home for the great adventure of his life's fortunes. Until then he had been the charge and anxiety of his elders, and under their rule and advice. Now he was free to choose; his was the power of direction, his the responsibility; for in the world one must be ranked by his own character and ability, and doomed by his own failures. The boy lifted his burden lightly, and turned with an eager smile to say farewell. But the old people and little Lydia were speechless with grief; they could not bear to part with the pride and hope and boyish strength, that were all their slender joy. The worn-out old man, the anxious woman who had been beaten and buffeted by the waves of poverty and sorrow, the little sister with her dreaming heart, stood at the bars and hungrily watched him go away. They feared success for him almost as much as failure. The world was before him now, with its treasures and pleasures, but with those inevitable disappointments and losses which old people know and fear; those sorrows of incapacity and lack of judgment which young hearts go out to meet without foreboding. It was a world of love and favor to which little Lydia's brother had gone; but who would know her fairy prince, in that disguise of a country boy's bashfulness and humble raiment from the cheap counter of a country store? The household stood rapt and silent until the farm wagon had made its last rise on the hilly road and disappeared.

"Well, he's left us now," said the sorrowful, hopeful old grandfather. "I expect I've got to turn to an' be a boy again myself. I feel to hope 'Lisha'll do as well as we covet for him. I seem to take it in, all my father felt when he let me go off to sea. He stood where I'm standin' now, an' I was just as triflin' as pore 'Lisha, and felt full as big as a man. But Lord! how I give up when it come night, an' I took it in I was gone from home!"

"There, don't ye, father," said the pale mother gently. She was, after all, the stronger of the two. "'Lisha's good an' honest-hearted. You'll feel real proud a year from now, when he gits back. I'm so glad he's got his watch to carry,—he did feel so grand. I expect them poor hens is sufferin'; nobody's thought on 'em this livin' mornin'. You'd better step an' feed 'em right away, sir." She could hardly speak for sorrow and excitement, but the old man was diverted at once, and hobbled away with cheerful importance on his two canes. Then she looked round at the poor, stony little farm almost angrily. "He'd no natural turn for the sea, 'Lisha hadn't; but I might have kept him with me if the land was good for anything."

Elisha felt as if lie were in a dream, now that his great adventure was begun. He answered John Sykes's questions mechanically, and his head was a little dull and dazed. Then he began to fear that the slow plodding of the farm horses would make him too late for the steamboat, and with sudden satisfaction pulled out the great watch to see if there were still time enough to get to the landing. He was filled with remorse because it was impossible to remember whether he had thanked Ma'am Stover for her gift. It seemed like a thing of life and consciousness as he pushed it back into his tight pocket. John Sykes looked at him curiously. "Why, that's old Ma'am Stover's timepiece, ain't it? Lend it to ye, did she?"

"Gave it to me," answered Elisha proudly.

"You be careful of that watch," said the driver soberly; and Elisha nodded.

"Well, good-day to ye; be a stiddy lad," advised John Sykes, a few minutes afterward. "Don't start in too smart an' scare 'm up to Boston. Pride an' ambition was the downfall o' old Cole's dog. There, sonny, the bo't ain't nowheres in sight, for all your fidgetin'!"

They both smiled broadly at the humorous warning, and as the old wagon rattled away, Elisha stood a moment looking after it; then he went down to the wharf by winding ways among piles of decayed timber and disused lobster-pots. A small group of travelers and spectators had already assembled, and they stared at him in a way that made him feel separated from his kind, though some of them had come to see him depart. One unenlightened acquaintance inquired if Elisha were expecting friends by that morning's boat; and when he explained that he was going away himself, asked kindly whether it was to be as far as Bath. Elisha mentioned the word "Boston" with scorn and compassion, but he did not feel like discussing his brilliant prospects now, as he had been more than ready to do the week before. Just then a deaf old woman asked for the time of day. She sat next him on the battered bench.

"Be you going up to Bath, dear?" she demanded suddenly; and he said yes. "Guess I'll stick to you, then, fur's you go; 't is kind o' blind in them big places." Elisha faintly nodded a meek but grudging assent; then, after a few moments, he boldly rose, tall umbrella in hand, and joined the talkative company of old and young men at the other side of the wharf. They proceeded to make very light of a person's going to Boston to enter upon his business career; but, after all, their thoughts were those of mingled respect and envy. Most of them had seen Boston, but no one save Elisha was going there that day to stay for a whole year. It made him feel like a city man.

The steamer whistled loud and hoarse before she came in sight, but presently the gay flags showed close by above the pointed spruces. Then she came jarring against the wharf, and the instant bustle and hurry, the strange faces of the passengers, and the loud rattle of freight going on board, were as confusing and exciting as if a small piece of Boston itself had been dropped into that quiet cove.

The people on the wharf shouted cheerful good-byes, to which the young traveler responded; then he seated himself well astern to enjoy the views, and felt as if he had made a thousand journeys. He bought a newspaper, and began to read it with much pride and a beating heart. The little old woman came and sat beside him, and talked straight on whether he listened or not, until he was afraid of what the other passengers might think, but nobody looked that way, and he could not find anything in the paper that he cared to read. Alone, but unfettered and aflame with courage; to himself he was not the boy who went away, but the proud man who one day would be coming home.

"Goin' to Boston, be ye?" asked the old lady for the third time; and it was still a pleasure to say yes, when the boat swung round, and there,

SARAH ORNE JEWETT

far away on its gray and green pasture slope, with the dark evergreens standing back, were the low gray house, and the little square barn, and the lines of fence that shut in his home. He strained his eyes to see if any one were watching from the door. He had almost forgotten that they could see him still. He sprang to the boat's side: yes, his mother remembered; there was something white waving from the doorway. The whole landscape faded from his eyes except that faraway gray house; his heart leaped back with love and longing; he gazed and gazed, until a height of green forest came between and shut the picture out. Then the country boy went on alone to make his way in the wide world.

IN DARK NEW ENGLAND DAYS

I

The last of the neighbors was going home; officious Mrs. Peter Downs had lingered late and sought for additional housework with which to prolong her stay. She had talked incessantly, and buzzed like a busy bee as she helped to put away the best crockery after the funeral supper, while the sisters Betsey and Hannah Knowles grew every moment more forbidding and unwilling to speak. They lighted a solitary small oil lamp at last, as if for Sunday evening idleness, and put it on the side table in the kitchen.

"We ain't intending to make a late evening of it," announced Betsey, the elder, standing before Mrs. Downs in an expectant, final way, making an irresistible opportunity for saying good-night. "I'm sure we're more than obleeged to ye,—ain't we, Hannah?—but I don't feel's if we ought to keep ye longer. We ain't going to do no more to-night, but set down a spell and kind of collect ourselves, and then make for bed."

Susan Downs offered one more plea. "I'd stop all night with ye an' welcome; 't is gettin' late—an' dark," she added plaintively; but the sisters shook their heads quickly, while Hannah said that they might as well get used to staying alone, since they would have to do it first or last. In spite of herself Mrs. Downs was obliged to put on her funeral best bonnet and shawl and start on her homeward way.

"Closed-mouthed old maids!" she grumbled as the door shut behind her all too soon and denied her the light of the lamp along the footpath. Suddenly there was a bright ray from the window, as if some one had pushed back the curtain and stood with the lamp close to the sash. "That's Hannah," said the retreating guest. "She'd told me somethin' about things, I know, if it hadn't 'a' been for Betsey. Catch me workin' myself to pieces again for 'em." But, however grudgingly this was said, Mrs. Downs's conscience told her that the industry of the past two days had been somewhat selfish on her part; she had hoped that in the excitement of this unexpected funeral season she might for once be taken into the sisters' confidence. More than this, she knew that they were certain of her motive, and had deliberately refused the expected satisfaction. "'T ain't as if I was one o' them curious busy-bodies anyway," she said to herself pityingly; "they might 'a' neighbored with somebody for once, I do believe." Everybody would have a question ready for her the next day, for it was known that she had been slaving herself devotedly since the news had come of old Captain Knowles's sudden death in his bed from a stroke, the last of three which had in the course of a year or two changed him from a strong old man to a feeble, chair-bound cripple.

Mrs. Downs stepped bravely along the dark country road; she could see a light in her own kitchen window half a mile away, and did not stop to notice either the penetrating dampness, or the shadowy woods at her right. It was a cloudy night, but there was a dim light over the open fields. She had a disposition of mind towards the exciting circumstances of death and burial, and was in request at such times among her neighbors; in this she was like a city person who prefers tragedy to comedy, but not having the semblance within her reach, she made the most of looking on at real griefs and departures.

Some one was walking towards her in the road; suddenly she heard footsteps. The figure stopped, then it came forward again.

"Oh, 't is you, ain't it?" with a tone of disappointment. "I cal'lated you'd stop all night, 't had got to be so late, an' I was just going over to the Knowles gals'; well, to kind o' ask how they be, an'"—Mr. Peter Downs was evidently counting on his visit.

"They never passed me the compliment," replied the wife. "I declare I didn't covet the walk home; I'm most beat out, bein' on foot so much. I was 'most put out with 'em for letten' of me see quite so plain that my room was better than my company. But I don't know's I blame 'em; they want to look an' see what they've got, an' kind of git by theirselves, I expect. 'T was natural."

Mrs. Downs knew that her husband would resent her first statements, being a sensitive and grumbling man. She had formed a pacific habit of suiting her remarks to his point of view, to save an outburst. He contented Himself with calling the Knowles girls hoggish, and put a direct question as to whether they had let fall any words about their situation, but Martha Downs was obliged to answer in the negative.

"Was Enoch Holt there after the folks come back from the grave?"

"He wa'n't; they never give *him* no encouragement neither."

"He appeared well, I must say," continued Peter Downs. "He took his place next but one behind us in the procession, 'long of Melinda Dutch, an' walked to an' from with her, give her his arm, and then I never see him after we got back; but I thought he might be somewhere in the house, an' I was out about the barn an' so on."

"They was civil to him. I was by when he come, just steppin' out of the bedroom after we'd finished layin' the old Cap'n into his coffin. Hannah looked real pleased when she see Enoch, as if she hadn't really expected him, but Betsey stuck out her hand's if 't was an eend o' board, an' drawed her face solemner 'n ever. There, they had natural feelin's. He was their own father when all was said, the Cap'n was, an' I don't know but he was clever to 'em in his way, 'ceptin' when he disappointed Hannah about her marryin' Jake Good'in. She l'arned to respect the old Cap'n's foresight, too."

"Sakes alive, Marthy, how you do knock folks down with one hand an' set 'em up with t' other," chuckled Mr. Downs. They next discussed the Captain's appearance as he lay in state in the front room, a subject which, with its endless ramifications, would keep the whole neighborhood interested for weeks to come.

An hour later the twinkling light in the Downs house suddenly disappeared. As Martha Downs took a last look out of doors through her bedroom window she could see no other light; the neighbors had all gone to bed. It was a little past nine, and the night was damp and still.

The Captain Knowles place was eastward from the Downs's, and a short turn in the road and the piece of hard-wood growth hid one house from the other. At this unwontedly late hour the elderly sisters were still sitting in their warm kitchen; there were bright coals under the singing tea-kettle which hung from the crane by three or four long pothooks. Betsey Knowles objected when her sister offered to put on more wood.

"Father never liked to leave no great of a fire, even though he slept right here in the bedroom. He said this floor was one that would light an' catch easy, you r'member."

"Another winter we can move down and take the bedroom ourselves—'t will be warmer for us," suggested Hannah; but Betsey shook her head doubtfully. The thought of their old father's grave, unwatched and undefended in the outermost dark field, filled their hearts with a strange tenderness. They had been his dutiful, patient slaves, and it seemed like disloyalty to have abandoned the poor shape; to be sitting there disregarding the thousand requirements and services of the past. More than all, they were facing a free future; they were their own mistresses at last, though past sixty years of age. Hannah was still a child at heart. She chased away a dread suspicion, when Betsey forbade the wood, lest this elder sister, who favored their father's looks, might take his place as stern ruler of the household.

"Betsey," said the younger sister suddenly, "we'll have us a cook stove, won't we, next winter? I expect we're going to have something to do with?"

Betsey did not answer; it was impossible to say whether she truly felt grief or only assumed it. She had been sober and silent for the most part since she routed neighbor Downs, though she answered her sister's prattling questions with patience and sympathy. Now, she rose from her chair and went to one of the windows, and, pushing back the sash curtain, pulled the wooden shutter across and hasped it.

"I ain't going to bed just yet," she explained. "I've been a-waiting to make sure nobody was coming in. I don't know's there'll be any better time to look in the chest and see what we've got to depend on. We never'll get no chance to do it by day."

Hannah looked frightened for a moment, then nodded, and turned to the opposite window and pulled that shutter with much difficulty; it had always caught and hitched and been provoking—a warped piece of red oak, when even-grained white pine would have saved strength and patience to three generations of the Knowles race. Then the sisters crossed the kitchen and opened the bedroom door. Hannah shivered a little as the colder air struck her, and her heart beat loudly. Perhaps it was the same with Betsey.

The bedroom was clean and orderly for the funeral guests. Instead of the blue homespun there was a beautifully quilted white coverlet which had been part of their mother's wedding furnishing, and this made the bedstead with its four low posts look unfamiliar and awesome. The lamplight shone through the kitchen door behind them, not very bright at best, but Betsey reached under the bed, and with all the strength she could muster pulled out the end of a great sea chest. The sisters tugged together and pushed, and made the most of their strength before they finally brought it through the narrow door into the kitchen. The solemnity of the deed made them both whisper as they talked, and Hannah did not dare to say what was in her timid heart—that she would rather brave discovery by daylight than such a feeling of being disapprovingly watched now, in the dead of night. There came a slight sound outside the house which made her look anxiously at Betsey, but Betsey remained tranquil.

"It's nothing but a stick falling down the woodpile," she answered in a contemptuous whisper, and the younger woman was reassured.

Betsey reached deep into her pocket and found a great key which was worn smooth and bright like silver, and never had been trusted willingly into even her own careful hands. Hannah held the lamp, and the two thin figures bent eagerly over the lid as it opened. Their shadows were waving about the low walls, and looked like strange shapes bowing and dancing behind them.

The chest was stoutly timbered, as if it were built in some ship-yard, and there were heavy wrought-iron hinges and a large escutcheon for the keyhole that the ship's blacksmith might have hammered out. On the top somebody had scratched deeply the crossed lines for a game of fox and geese, which had a trivial, irreverent look, and might have been the unforgiven fault of some idle ship's boy. The sisters had hardly dared look at the chest or to signify their knowledge of its existence, at unwary times. They had swept carefully about it year after year, and wondered if it were indeed full of gold as the neighbors used to hint; but no matter how much found a way in, little had found the way out. They had been hampered all their lives for money, and in consequence had developed a wonderful facility for spinning and weaving, mending and making. Their small farm was an early example of intensive farming; they were allowed to use its products in a niggardly way, but the money that was paid for wool, for hay, for wood, and for summer crops had all gone into the chest. The old captain was a hard master; he rarely commended and often blamed. Hannah trembled before him, but Betsey faced him sturdily, being amazingly like him, with a feminine difference; as like as a ruled person can be to a ruler, for the discipline of life had taught the man to aggress, the woman only to defend. In the chest was a fabled sum of prize-money, besides these slender earnings of many years; all the sisters' hard work and self-sacrifice were there in money and a mysterious largess besides. All their lives they had been looking forward to this hour of ownership.

There was a solemn hush in the house; the two sisters were safe from their neighbors, and there was no fear of interruption at such an hour in that hard-working community, tired with a day's work that had been early begun. If any one came knocking at the door, both door and windows were securely fastened.

The eager sisters bent above the chest, they held their breath and talked in softest whispers. With stealthy tread a man came out of the woods near by.

He stopped to listen, came nearer, stopped again, and then crept close to the old house. He stepped upon the banking, next the window with the warped shutter; there was a knothole in it high above the women's heads, towards the top. As they leaned over the chest, an eager eye watched them. If they had turned that way suspiciously, the eye might have caught the flicker of the lamp and betrayed itself. No, they were too busy: the eye at the shutter watched and watched.

There was a certain feeling of relief in the sisters' minds because the contents of the chest were so commonplace at first sight. There were some old belongings dating back to their father's early days of seafaring. They unfolded a waistcoat pattern or two of figured stuff which they had seen him fold and put away again and again. Once he had given Betsey a gay China silk handkerchief, and here were two more like it. They had not known what a store of treasures might be waiting for them, but the reality so far was disappointing; there was much spare room to begin with, and the wares within looked pinched and few. There were bundles of papers, old receipts, some letters in two not very thick bundles, some old account books with worn edges, and a blackened silver can which looked very small in comparison with their anticipation, being an heirloom and jealously hoarded and secreted by the old man. The women began to feel as if his lean angry figure were bending with them over the sea chest.

They opened a package wrapped in many layers of old soft paper—a worked piece of Indian muslin, and an embroidered red scarf which they had never seen before. "He must have brought them home to mother," said Betsey with a great outburst of feeling. "He never was the same man again; he never would let nobody else have them when he found she was dead, poor old father!"

Hannah looked wistfully at the treasures. She rebuked herself for selfishness, but she thought of her pinched girlhood and the delight these things would have been. Ah yes! it was too late now for many things besides the sprigged muslin. "If I was young as I was once there's lots o' things I'd like to do now I'm free," said Hannah with a gentle sigh; but her sister checked her anxiously—it was fitting that they should preserve a semblance of mourning even to themselves.

The lamp stood in a kitchen chair at the chest's end and shone full across their faces. Betsey looked intent and sober as she turned over the old man's treasures. Under the India mull was an antique pair of buff trousers, a waistcoat of strange old-fashioned foreign stuff, and a blue coat with brass buttons, brought home from over seas, as the women knew, for their father's wedding clothes. They had seen him carry them out at long intervals to hang them in the spring sunshine; he had been very feeble the last time, and Hannah remembered that she had longed to take them from his shaking hands.

"I declare for't I wish't we had laid him out in 'em, 'stead o' the robe," she whispered; but Betsey made no answer. She was kneeling still, but held herself upright and looked away. It was evident that she was lost in her own thoughts.

"I can't find nothing else by eyesight," she muttered. "This chest never'd be so heavy with them old clothes. Stop! Hold that light down, Hannah; there's a place underneath here. Them papers in the till takes a shallow part. Oh, my gracious! See here, will ye? Hold the light, hold the light!"

There was a hidden drawer in the chest's side—a long, deep place, and it was full of gold pieces. Hannah had seated herself in the chair to be out of her sister's way. She held the lamp with one hand and gathered her apron on her lap with the other, while Betsey, exultant and hawk-eyed, took out handful after handful of heavy coins, letting them jingle and chink, letting them shine in the lamp's rays, letting them roll across the floor—guineas, dollars, doubloons, old French and Spanish and English gold!

Now, now! Look! The eye at the window!

At last they have found it all; the bag of silver, the great roll of bank bills, and the heavy weight of gold—the prize-money that had been like Robinson Crusoe's in the cave. They were rich women that night; their faces grew young again as they sat side by side and exulted while the old kitchen grew cold. There was nothing they might not do within the range of their timid ambitions; they were women of fortune now and their own mistresses. They were beginning at last to live.

The watcher outside was cramped and chilled. He let himself down softly from the high step of the winter banking, and crept toward the barn, where he might bury himself in the hay and think. His fingers were quick to find the peg that opened the little barn door; the beasts within were startled and stumbled to their feet, then went back to their slumbers. The night wore on; the light spring rain began to fall, and the sound of it on the house roof close down upon the sisters' bed lulled them quickly to sleep. Twelve, one, two o'clock passed by.

They had put back the money and the clothes and the minor goods and treasures and pulled the chest back into the bedroom so that it was out of sight from the kitchen; the bedroom door was always shut by day. The younger sister wished to carry the money to their own room, but Betsey disdained such precaution. The money had always been safe in the old chest, and there it should stay. The next week they would go to Riverport and put it into the bank; it was no use to lose the interest any longer. Because their father had lost some invested money in his early youth, it did not follow that every bank was faithless. Betsey's self-assertion was amazing, but they still whispered to each other as they got ready for bed. With strange forgetfulness Betsey had laid the chest key on the white coverlet in the bedroom and left it there.

III

In August of that year the whole countryside turned out to go to court. The sisters had been rich for one night; in the morning they waked to find themselves poor with a bitter pang of poverty of which they had never dreamed. They had said little, but they grew suddenly pinched and old. They could not tell how much money they had lost, except that Hannah's lap was full of gold, a weight she could not lift nor carry. After a few days of stolid misery they had gone to the chief lawyer of their neighborhood to accuse Enoch Holt of the robbery. They dressed in their best and walked solemnly side by side across the fields and along the road, the shortest way to the man of law. Enoch Holt's daughter saw them go as she stood in her doorway, and felt a cold shiver run through her frame as if in foreboding. Her father was not at home; he had left for Boston late on the afternoon of Captain Knowles's funeral. He had had notice the day before of the coming in of a ship in which he owned a thirty-second; there was talk of selling the ship, and the owners' agent had summoned him. He had taken pains to go to the funeral, because he and the old captain had been on bad terms ever since they had bought a piece of woodland together, and the captain declared himself wronged at the settling of accounts. He was growing feeble even then, and had left the business to the younger man. Enoch Holt was not a trusted man, yet he had never before been openly accused of dishonesty. He was not a professor of religion, but foremost on the secular side of church matters. Most of the men in that region were hard men; it was difficult to get money, and there was little real comfort in a community where the sterner, stingier, forbidding side of New England life was well exemplified.

The proper steps had been taken by the officers of the law, and in answer to the writ Enoch Holt appeared, much shocked and very indignant, and was released on bail which covered the sum his shipping interest had brought him. The weeks had dragged by; June and July were long in passing, and here was court day at last, and all the townsfolk hastening by high-roads and by-roads to the court-house. The Knowles girls themselves had risen at break of day and walked the distance steadfastly, like two of the three Fates: who would make the third, to cut the thread for their enemy's disaster? Public opinion was divided. There were many voices ready to speak on the accused man's side; a sharp-looking acquaintance left his business in Boston to swear that Holt was in his office before noon on the day following the robbery, and that he had spent most of the night in Boston, as proved by several minor details of their interview. As for Holt's young married daughter, she was a favorite with the townsfolk, and her husband was away at sea overdue these last few weeks. She sat on one of the hard court benches with a young child in her arms, born since its father sailed; they had been more or less unlucky, the Holt family, though Enoch himself was a man of brag and bluster.

All the hot August morning, until the noon recess, and all the hot August afternoon, fly-teased and wretched with the heavy air, the crowd of neighbors listened to the trial. There was not much evidence brought; everybody knew that Enoch Holt left the funeral procession hurriedly, and went away on horseback towards Boston. His daughter knew no more than this. The Boston man gave his testimony impatiently, and one or two persons insisted that they saw the accused on his way at nightfall, several miles from home.

As the testimony came out, it all tended to prove his innocence, though public opinion was to the contrary. The Knowles sisters looked more stern and gray hour by hour; their vengeance was not to be satisfied; their accusation had been listened to and found wanting, but their instinctive knowledge of the matter counted for nothing. They must have been watched through the knot-hole of the shutter; nobody had noticed it until, some years before, Enoch Holt himself had spoken of the light's shining through on a winter's night as he came towards the house. The chief proof was that nobody else could have done the deed. But why linger over *pros* and *cons?* The jury returned directly with a verdict of "not proven," and the tired audience left the court-house.

But not until Hannah Knowles with angry eyes had risen to her feet.

The sterner elder sister tried to pull her back; every one said that they should have looked to Betsey to say the awful words that followed, not to her gentler companion. It was Hannah, broken and disappointed, who cried in a strange high voice as Enoch Holt was passing by without a look:

"You stole it, you thief! You know it in your heart!"

The startled man faltered, then he faced the women. The people who stood near seemed made of eyes as they stared to see what he would say.

"I swear by my right hand I never touched it."

"Curse your right hand, then!" cried Hannah Knowles, growing tall and thin like a white flame drawing upward. "Curse your right hand, yours and all your folks' that follow you! May I live to see the day!"

The people drew back, while for a moment accused and accuser stood face to face. Then Holt's flushed face turned white, and he shrank from the fire in those wild eyes, and walked away clumsily down the courtroom. Nobody followed him, nobody shook hands with him, or told the acquitted man that they were glad of his release. Half an hour later, Betsey and Hannah Knowles took their homeward way, to begin their hard round of work again. The horizon that had widened with such glory for one night, had closed round them again like an iron wall.

Betsey was alarmed and excited by her sister's uncharacteristic behavior, and she looked at her anxiously from time to time. Hannah had become the harder-faced of the two. Her disappointment was the keener, for she had kept more of the unsatisfied desires of her girlhood until that dreary morning when they found the sea-chest rifled and the treasure gone.

Betsey said inconsequently that it was a pity she did not have that black silk gown that would stand alone. They had planned for it over the open chest, and Hannah's was to be a handsome green. They might have worn them to court. But even the pathetic facetiousness of her elder sister did not bring a smile to Hannah Knowles's face, and the next day one was at the loom and the other at the wheel again. The neighbors talked about the curse with horror; in their minds a fabric of sad fate was spun from the bitter words.

The Knowles sisters never had worn silk gowns and they never would. Sometimes Hannah or Betsey would stealthily look over the chest in one or the other's absence. One day when Betsey was very old and her mind had grown feeble, she tied her own India silk handkerchief about her neck, but they never used the other two. They aired the wedding suit once every spring as long as they lived. They were both too old and forlorn to make up the India mull. Nobody knows how many times they took everything out of the heavy old clamped box, and peered into every nook and corner to see if there was not a single gold piece left. They never answered any one who made bold to speak of their misfortune.

IV

Enoch Holt had been a seafaring man in his early days, and there was news that the owners of a Salem ship in which he held a small interest wished him to go out as supercargo. He was brisk and well in health, and his son-in-law, an honest but an unlucky fellow, had done less well than usual, so that nobody was surprised when Enoch made ready for his voyage. It was nearly a year after the theft, and nothing had come so near to restoring him to public favor as his apparent lack of ready money. He openly said that he put great hope in his adventure to the Spice Islands, and when he said farewell one Sunday to some members of the dispersing congregation, more than one person wished him heartily a pleasant voyage and safe return. He had an insinuating tone of voice and an imploring look that day, and this fact, with his probable long absence and the dangers of the deep, won him much sympathy. It is a shameful thing to accuse a man wrongfully, and Enoch Holt had behaved well since the trial; and, what is more, had shown no accession to his means of living. So away he went, with a fair amount of good wishes, though one or two persons assured remonstrating listeners that they thought it likely Enoch would make a good voyage, better than common, and show himself forwarded when he came to port. Soon after his departure, Mrs. Peter Downs and an intimate acquaintance discussed the ever-exciting subject of the Knowles robbery over a friendly cup of tea.

They were in the Downs kitchen, and quite by themselves. Peter Downs himself had been drawn as a juror, and had been for two days at the county town. Mrs. Downs was giving herself to social interests in his absence, and Mrs. Forder, an asthmatic but very companionable person, had arrived by two o'clock that afternoon with her knitting work, sure of being welcome. The two old friends had first talked over varied subjects of immediate concern, but when supper was nearly finished, they fell back upon the lost Knowles gold, as has been already said.

"They got a dreadful blow, poor gals," wheezed Mrs. Forder, with compassion. "'T was harder for them than for most folks; they'd had a long stent with the ol' gentleman; very arbitrary, very arbitrary."

"Yes," answered Mrs. Downs, pushing back her tea-cup, then lifting it again to see if it was quite empty. "Yes, it took holt o' Hannah, the most. I should 'a' said Betsey was a good deal the most set in her ways an' would 'a' been most tore up, but 't wa'n't so."

"Lucky that Holt's folks sets on the other aisle in the meetin'-house, I do consider, so 't they needn't face each other sure as Sabbath comes round."

"I see Hannah an' him come face to face two Sabbaths afore Enoch left. So happened he dallied to have a word 'long o' Deacon Good'in, an' him an' Hannah stepped front of each other 'fore they knowed what they's about. I sh'd thought her eyes 'd looked right through him. No one of 'em took the word; Enoch he slinked off pretty quick."

"I see 'em too," said Mrs. Forder; "made my blood run cold."

"Nothin' ain't come of the curse yit,"—Mrs. Downs lowered the tone of her voice,—"least, folks says so. It kind o' worries pore Phoebe Holt— Mis' Dow, I would say. She was narved all up at the time o' the trial, an' when her next baby come into the world, first thin' she made out t' ask me was whether it seemed likely, an' she gived me a pleadin' look as if I'd got to tell her what she hadn't heart to ask. 'Yes, dear,' says I, 'put up his little hands to me kind of wonted'; an' she turned a look on me like another creatur', so pleased an' contented."

"I s'pose you don't see no great of the Knowles gals?" inquired Mrs. Forder, who lived two miles away in the other direction.

"They stepped to the door yesterday when I was passin' by, an' I went in an' set a spell long of 'em," replied the hostess. "They'd got pestered with that ol' loom o' theirn. 'Fore I thought, says I, ''T is all worn out, Betsey,' says I. 'Why on airth don't ye git somebody to git some o' your own wood an' season it well so 't won't warp, same's mine done, an' build ye a new one?' But Betsey muttered an' twitched away; 't wa'n't like her, but they're dis'p'inted at every turn, I s'pose, an' feel poor where they've got the same's ever to do with. Hannah's a-coughin' this spring's if somethin' ailed her. I asked her if she had bad feelin's in her pipes, an' she said yis, she had, but not to speak of 't before Betsey. I'm goin' to fix her up some hoarhound an' elecampane quick's the ground's nice an' warm an' roots livens up a grain more. They're limp an' wizened 'long to the fust of the spring. Them would be service'ble, simmered away to a syrup 'long o' molasses; now don't you think so, Mis' Forder?"

"Excellent," replied the wheezing dame. "I covet a portion myself, now you speak. Nothin' cures my complaint, but a new remedy takes holt clever sometimes, an' eases me for a spell." And she gave a plaintive sigh, and began to knit again.

Mrs. Downs rose and pushed the supper-table to the wall and drew her chair nearer to the stove. The April nights were chilly.

"The folks is late comin' after me," said Mrs. Forder, ostentatiously. "I may's well confess that I told 'em if they was late with the work they might let go o' fetchin' o' me an' I'd walk home in the mornin'; take it easy when I was fresh. Course I mean ef 't wouldn't put you out: I knowed you was all alone, an' I kind o' wanted a change."

"Them words was in my mind to utter while we was to table," avowed Mrs. Downs, hospitably. "I ain't reely afeared, but 't is sort o' creepy fastenin' up an' goin' to bed alone. Nobody can't help hearkin', an' every common noise starts you. I never used to give nothin' a thought till the Knowleses was robbed, though."

"'T was mysterious, I do maintain," acknowledged Mrs. Forder. "Comes over me sometimes p'raps 't wasn't Enoch; he'd 'a' branched out more in course o' time. I'm waitin' to see if he does extry well to sea 'fore I let my mind come to bear on his bein' clean handed."

"Plenty thought 't was the ole Cap'n come back for it an' sperited it away. Enough said that 't wasn't no honest gains; most on't was prize-money o' slave ships, an' all kinds o' devil's gold was mixed in. I s'pose you've heard that said?"

"Time an' again," responded Mrs. Forder; "an' the worst on't was simple old Pappy Flanders went an' told the Knowles gals themselves that folks thought the ole Cap'n come back an' got it, and Hannah done wrong to cuss Enoch Holt an' his ginerations after him the way she done."

"I think it took holt on her ter'ble after all she'd gone through," said Mrs. Downs, compassionately. "He ain't near so simple as he is ugly, Pappy Flanders ain't. I've seen him set here an' read the paper sober's anybody when I've been goin' about my mornin's work in the shed-room, an' when I'd come in to look about he'd twist it with his hands an' roll his eyes an' begin to git off some o' his gable. I think them wander-in' cheap-wits likes the fun on't an' 'scapes stiddy work, an' gits the rovin' habit so fixed, it sp'iles 'em."

"My gran'ther was to the South Seas in his young days," related Mrs. Forder, impressively, "an' he said cussin' was common there. I mean sober spitin' with a cuss. He seen one o' them black folks git a gredge against another an' go an' set down an' look stiddy at him in his hut an' cuss him in his mind an' set there an' watch, watch, until the other kind o' took sick an' died, all in a fortnight, I believe he said; 't would make your blood run cold to hear gran'ther describe it, 't would so. He never done nothin' but set an' look, an' folks would give him somethin' to eat now an' then, as if they thought 't was all right, an' the other one 'd try to go an' come, an' at last he hived away altogether an' died. I don't know what you'd call it that ailed him. There's suthin' in cussin' that's bad for folks, now I tell ye, Mis' Downs."

"Hannah's eyes always makes me creepy now," Mrs. Downs confessed uneasily. "They don't look pleadin' an' childish same 's they used to. Seems to me as if she'd had the worst on't."

"We ain't seen the end on't yit," said Mrs. Forder, impressively. "I feel it within me, Marthy Downs, an' it's a terrible thing to have happened right amon'st us in Christian times. If we live long enough we're goin' to have plenty to talk over in our old age that's come o' that cuss. Some seed's shy o' sproutin' till a spring when the s'ile's jest right to breed it."

"There's lobeely now," agreed Mrs. Downs, pleased to descend to prosaic and familiar levels. "They ain't a good crop one year in six, and then you find it in a place where you never observed none to grow afore, like's not; ain't it so, reelly?" And she rose to clear the table, pleased with the certainty of a guest that night. Their conversation was not reassuring to the heart of a timid woman, alone in an isolated farmhouse on a dark spring evening, especially so near the anniversary of old Captain Knowles's death.

V

Later in these rural lives by many years two aged women were crossing a wide field together, following a footpath such as one often finds between widely separated homes of the New England country. Along these lightly traced thoroughfares, the children go to play, and lovers to plead, and older people to companion one another in work and pleasure, in sickness and sorrow; generation after generation comes and goes again by these country by-ways.

The footpath led from Mrs. Forder's to another farmhouse half a mile beyond, where there had been a wedding. Mrs. Downs was there, and in the June weather she had been easily persuaded to go home to tea with Mrs. Forder with the promise of being driven home later in the evening. Mrs. Downs's husband had been dead three years, and her friend's large family was scattered from the old nest; they were lonely at times in their later years, these old friends, and found it very pleasant now to have a walk together. Thin little Mrs. Forder, with all her wheezing, was the stronger and more active of the two: Downs had grown heavier and weaker with advancing years.

They paced along the footpath slowly, Mrs. Downs rolling in her gait like a sailor, and availing herself of every pretext to stop and look at herbs in the pasture ground they crossed, and at the growing grass in the mowing fields. They discussed the wedding minutely, and then where the way grew wider they walked side by side instead of following each other, and their voices sank to the low tone that betokens confidence.

"You don't say that you really put faith in all them old stories?"

"It ain't accident altogether, noways you can fix it in your mind," maintained Mrs. Downs. "Needn't tell me that cussin' don't do neither good nor harm. I shouldn't want to marry amon'st the Holts if I was young ag'in! I r'member when this young man was born that's married to-day, an' the fust thing his poor mother wanted to know was about his hands bein' right. I said yes they was, but las' year he was twenty year old and come home from the frontier with one o' them hands—his right one—shot off in a fight. They say 't happened to sights o' other fel-lows, an' their laigs gone too, but I count 'em over on my fingers, them Holts, an' he's the third. May say 't was all an accident his mother's gittin' throwed out o' her waggin comin' home from meetin', an' her wrist not bein' set good, an' she, bein' run down at the time, 'most lost it altogether, but thar' it is, stiffened up an' no good to her. There was the second. An' Enoch Holt hisself come home from the Chiny seas, made a good passage an' a sight o' money in the pepper trade, jest's we expected, an' goin' to build him a new house, an' the frame gives a kind o' lurch when they was raisin' of it an' surges over on to him an' nips him under. 'Which arm?' says everybody along the road when they was comin' an' goin' with the doctor. 'Right one—got to lose it,' says the doctor to 'em, an' next time Enoch Holt got out to meetin' he stood up in the house o' God with the hymn-book in his left hand, an' no right hand to turn his leaf with. He knowed what we was all a-thinkin'."

"Well," said Mrs. Forder, very short-breathed with climbing the long slope of the pasture hill, "I don't know but I'd as soon be them as the Knowles gals. Hannah never knowed no peace again after she spoke them words in the co't-house. They come back an' harnted her, an' you know, Miss Downs, better 'n I do, being door-neighbors as one may say, how they lived their lives out like wild beasts into a lair."

"They used to go out some by night to git the air," pursued Mrs. Downs with interest. "I used to open the door an' step right in, an' I used to take their yarn an' stuff 'long o' mine an' sell 'em, an' do for the poor stray creatur's long's they'd let me. They'd be grateful for a mess o' early pease or potatoes as ever you see, an' Peter he allays favored 'em with pork, fresh an' salt, when we slaughtered. The old Cap'n kept 'em child'n long as he lived, an' then they was too old to l'arn different. I allays liked Hannah the best till that change struck her. Betsey she held out to the last jest about the same. I don't know, now I come to think of it, but what she felt it the most o' the two."

"They'd never let me's much as git a look at 'em," complained Mrs. Forder. "Folks got awful stories a-goin' one time. I've heard it said, an' it allays creeped me cold all over, that there was somethin' come an' lived with 'em—a kind o' black shadder, a cobweb kind o' a man-shape that followed 'em about the house an' made a third to them; but they got hardened to it theirselves, only they was afraid 't would follow if they went anywheres from home. You don't believe no such piece o' nonsense?—But there, I've asked ye times enough before."

"They'd got shadders enough, poor creatur's," said Mrs. Downs with reserve. "Wasn't no kind o' need to make 'em up no spooks, as I know on. Well, here's these young folks a-startin'; I wish 'em well, I'm sure. She likes him with his one hand better than most gals likes them as has a good sound pair. They looked prime happy; I hope no curse won't foller 'em."

The friends stopped again—poor, short-winded bodies—on the crest of the low hill and turned to look at the wide landscape, bewildered by the marvelous beauty and the sudden flood of golden sunset light that poured out of the western sky. They could not remember that they had ever observed the wide view before; it was like a revelation or an outlook towards the celestial country, the sight of their own green farms and the countryside that bounded them. It was a pleasant country indeed, their own New England: their petty thoughts and vain imaginings seemed futile and unrelated to so fair a scene of things. But the figure of a man who was crossing the meadow below looked like a malicious black insect. It was an old man, it was Enoch Holt; time had worn and bent him enough to have satisfied his bitterest foe. The women could see his empty coat-sleeve flutter as he walked slowly and unexpectantly in that glorious evening light.

THE WHITE ROSE ROAD

B eing a New Englander, it is natural that I should first speak about the weather. Only the middle of June, the green fields, and blue sky, and bright sun, with a touch of northern mountain wind blowing straight toward the sea, could make such a day, and that is all one can say about it. We were driving seaward through a part of the country which has been least changed in the last thirty years,—among farms which have been won from swampy lowland, and rocky, stamp-buttressed hillsides: where the forests wall in the fields, and send their outposts year by year farther into the pastures. There is a year or two in the history of these pastures before they have arrived at the dignity of being called woodland, and yet are too much shaded and overgrown by young trees to give proper pasturage, when they made delightful harbors for the small wild creatures which yet remain, and for wild flowers and berries. Here you send an astonished rabbit scurrying to his burrow, and there you startle yourself with a partridge, who seems to get the best of the encounter. Sometimes you see a hen partridge and her brood of chickens crossing your path with an air of comfortable door-yard security. As you drive along the narrow, grassy road, you see many charming sights and delightful nooks on either hand, where the young trees spring out of a close-cropped turf that carpets the ground like velvet. Toward the east and the quaint fishing village of Ogunquit, I find the most delightful woodland roads. There is little left of the large timber which once filled the region, but much young growth, and there are hundreds of acres of cleared land and pasture-ground where the forests are springing fast and covering the country once more, as if they had no idea of losing in their war with civilization and the intruding white settler. The pine woods and the Indians seem to be next of kin, and the former owners of this corner of New England are the only proper figures to paint into such landscapes. The twilight under tall pines seems to be untenanted and to lack something, at first sight, as if one opened the door of an empty house. A farmer passing through with his axe is but an intruder, and children straying home from school give one a feeling of solicitude at their unprotectedness. The pine woods are the red man's house, and it may be hazardous even yet for the gray farmhouses to stand so near the eaves of the forest. I have noticed a distrust of the deep woods, among elderly people, which was something more than a fear of losing their way. It was a feeling of defenselessness against some unrecognized but malicious influence.

Driving through the long woodland way, shaded and chilly when you are out of the sun; across the Great Works River and its pretty elm-grown intervale; across the short bridges of brown brooks; delayed now and then by the sight of ripe strawberries in sunny spots by the roadside, one comes to a higher open country, where farm joins farm, and the cleared fields lie all along the highway, while the woods are pushed back a good distance on either hand. The wooded hills, bleak here and there with granite ledges, rise beyond. The houses are beside the road, with green door-yards and large barns, almost empty now, and with wide doors standing open, as if they were already expecting the hay crop to be brought in. The tall green grass is waving in the fields as the wind goes over, and there is a fragrance of whiteweed and ripe strawberries and clover blowing through the sunshiny barns, with their lean sides and their festoons of brown, dusty cobwebs; dull, comfortable creatures they appear to imaginative eyes, waiting hungrily for their yearly meal. The eave-swallows are teasing their sleepy shapes, like the birds which flit about great beasts; gay, movable, irreverent, almost derisive, those barn swallows fly to and fro in the still, clear air.

The noise of our wheels brings fewer faces to the windows than usual, and we lose the pleasure of seeing some of our friends who are apt to be looking out, and to whom we like to say good-day. Some funeral must be taking place, or perhaps the women may have gone out into the fields. It is hoeing-time and strawberry-time, and already we have seen some of the younger women at work among the corn and potatoes. One sight will be charming to remember. On a green hillside sloping to the west, near one of the houses, a thin little girl was working away lustily with a big hoe on a patch of land perhaps fifty feet by twenty. There were all sorts of things growing there, as if a child's fancy had made the choice,—straight rows of turnips and carrots and beets, a little of everything, one might say; but the only touch of color was from a long border of useful sage in full bloom of dull blue, on the upper side. I am sure this was called Katy's or Becky's *piece* by the elder members of the family. One can imagine how the young creature had planned it in the spring, and persuaded the men to plough and harrow it, and since then had stoutly done all the work herself, and meant to send the harvest of the piece to market, and pocket her honest gains, as they came in, for some great end. She was as thin as a grasshopper, this busy little gardener, and hardly turned to give us a glance, as we drove slowly up the hill close by. The sun will brown and dry her like a spear of grass on that hot slope, but a spark of fine spirit is in the small body, and I wish her a famous crop. I hate to say that the piece looked backward, all except the sage, and that it was a heavy bit of land for the clumsy hoe to pick at. The only puzzle is, what she proposes to do with so long a row of sage. Yet there may be a large family with a downfall of measles yet ahead, and she does not mean to be caught without sage-tea.

Along this road every one of the old farmhouses has at least one tall bush of white roses by the door,—a most lovely sight, with buds and blossoms, and unvexed green leaves. I wish that I knew the history of them, and whence the first bush was brought. Perhaps from England itself, like a red rose that I know in Kittery, and the new shoots from the root were given to one neighbor after another all through the district. The bushes are slender, but they grow tall without climbing against the wall, and sway to and fro in the wind with a grace of youth and an inexpressible charm of beauty. How many lovers must have picked them on Sunday evenings, in all the bygone years, and carried them along the roads or by the pasture footpaths, hiding them clumsily under their Sunday coats if they caught sight of any one coming. Here, too, where the sea wind nips many a young life before its prime, how often the white roses have been put into paler hands, and withered there! In spite of the serene and placid look of the old houses, one who has always known them cannot help thinking of the sorrows of these farms and their almost undiverted toil. Near the little gardener's plot, we turned from the main road and drove through lately cleared woodland up to an old farmhouse, high on a ledgy hill, whence there is a fine view of the country seaward and mountain-ward. There were few of the once large household left there: only the old farmer, who was crippled by war wounds, active, cheerful man that he was once, and two young orphan children. There has been much hard work spent on the place. Every generation has toiled from youth to age without being able to make much beyond a living. The dollars that can be saved are but few, and sickness and death have often brought their bitter cost. The mistress of the farm was helpless for many years; through all the summers and winters she sat in her pillowed rocking-chair in the plain room. She could watch the seldom-visited lane, and beyond it, a little way across the fields, were the woods; besides these, only the clouds in the sky. She could not lift her food to her mouth; she could not be her husband's working partner. She never went into another woman's house to see her works and ways, but sat there, aching and tired, vexed by flies and by heat, and isolated in long storms. Yet the whole countryside neighbored her with true affection. Her spirit grew stronger as her body grew weaker, and the doctors, who grieved because they could do so little with their skill, were never confronted by that malady of the spirit, a desire for ease and laziness, which makes the soundest of bodies useless and complaining. The thought of her blooms in one's mind like the whitest of flowers; it makes one braver and more thankful to remember the simple faith and patience with which she bore her pain and trouble. How often she must have said, "I wish I could do something for you in return," when she was doing a thousand times more than if, like her neighbors, she followed the simple round of daily life! She was doing constant kindness by her example; but nobody can tell the woe of her long days and nights, the solitude of her spirit, as she was being lifted by such hard ways to the knowledge of higher truth and experience. Think of her pain when, one after another, her children fell ill and died, and she could not tend them! And now, in the same worn chair where she lived and slept sat her husband, helpless too, thinking of her, and missing her more than if she had been sometimes away from home, like other women. Even a stranger would miss her in the house.

There sat the old farmer looking down the lane in his turn, bearing his afflictions with a patient sternness that may have been born of watching his wife's serenity. There was a half-withered rose lying within his reach. Some days nobody came up the lane, and the wild birds that ventured near the house and the clouds that blew over were his only entertainment. He had a fine face, of the older New England type, clean-shaven and strong-featured,—a type that is fast passing away. He might have been a Cumberland dalesman, such were his dignity, and self-possession, and English soberness of manner. His large frame was built for hard work, for lifting great weights and pushing his plough through new-cleared land. We felt at home together, and each knew many things that the other did of earlier days, and of losses that had come with time. I remembered coming to the old house often in my childhood; it was in this very farm lane that I first saw anemones, and learned what to call them. After we drove away, this crippled man must have thought a long time about my elders and betters, as if he were reading their story out of a book. I suppose he has hauled many a stick of timber pine down for ship-yards, and gone through the village so early in the winter morning that I, waking in my warm bed, only heard the sleds creak through the frozen snow as the slow oxen plodded by.

Near the house a trout brook comes plashing over the ledges. At one place there is a most exquisite waterfall, to which neither painter's brush nor writer's pen can do justice. The sunlight falls through flickering leaves into the deep glen, and makes the foam whiter and the brook more golden-brown. You can hear the merry noise of it all night, all day, in the house. A little way above the farmstead it comes through marshy ground, which I fear has been the cause of much illness and sorrow to the poor, troubled family. I had a thrill of pain, as it seemed to me that the brook was mocking at all that trouble with all its wild carelessness and loud laughter, as it hurried away down the glen.

When we had said good-by and were turning the horses away, there suddenly appeared in a footpath that led down from one of the green hills the young grandchild, just coming home from school. She was as quick as a bird, and as shy in her little pink gown, and balanced herself on one foot, like a flower. The brother was the elder of the two orphans; he was the old man's delight and dependence by day, while his hired man was afield. The sober country boy had learned to wait and tend, and the young people were indeed a joy in that lonely household. There was no sign that they ever played like other children,—no truckle-cart in the yard, no doll, no bits of broken crockery in order on a rock. They had learned a fashion of life from their elders, and already could lift and carry their share of the burdens of life.

It was a country of wild flowers; the last of the columbines were clinging to the hillsides; down in the small, fenced meadows belonging to the farm were meadow rue just coming in flower, and red and white clover; the golden buttercups were thicker than the grass, while many mulleins were standing straight and slender among the pine stumps, with their first blossoms atop. Rudbeckias had found their way in, and appeared more than ever like bold foreigners. Their names should be translated into country speech, and the children ought to call them "rude-beckies," by way of relating them to bouncing-bets and sweet-williams. The pasture grass was green and thick after the plentiful rains, and the busy cattle took little notice of us as they browsed steadily and tinkled their pleasant bells. Looking off, the smooth, round back of Great Hill caught the sunlight with its fields of young grain, and all the long, wooded slopes and valleys were fresh and fair in the June weather, away toward the blue New Hampshire hills on the northern horizon. Seaward stood Agamenticus, dark with its pitch pines, and the far sea itself, blue and calm, ruled the uneven country with its unchangeable line.

Out on the white rose road again, we saw more of the rose-trees than ever, and now and then a carefully tended flower garden, always delightful to see and think about. These are not made by merely looking through a florist's catalogue, and ordering this or that new seedling and a proper selection of bulbs or shrubs; everything in a country garden has its history and personal association. The old bushes, the perennials, are apt to have most tender relationship with the hands that planted them long ago. There is a constant exchange of such treasures between the neighbors, and in the spring, slips and cuttings may be seen rooting on the window ledges, while the house plants give endless work all winter long, since they need careful protection against frost in long nights of the severe weather. A flower-loving woman brings back from every one of her infrequent journeys some treasure of flower-seeds or a huge miscellaneous nosegay. Time to work in the little plot of pleasure-ground is hardly won by the busy mistress of the farmhouse. The most appealing collection of flowering plants and vines that I ever saw was in Virginia, once, above the exquisite valley spanned by the Natural Bridge, a valley far too little known or praised. I had noticed an old log house, as I learned to know the outlook from the picturesque hotel, and was sure that it must give a charming view from its perch on the summit of a hill.

One day I went there,—one April day, when the whole landscape was full of color from the budding trees,—and before I could look at the view, I caught sight of some rare vines, already in leaf, about the dilapidated walls of the cabin. Then across the low paling I saw the brilliant colors of tulips and daffodils. There were many rose-bushes; in fact, the whole top of the hill was a flower garden, once well cared for and carefully ordered. It was all the work of an old woman of Scotch-Irish descent, who had been busy with the cares of life, and a very hard worker; yet I was told that to gratify her love for flowers she would often go afoot many miles over those rough Virginia roads, with a root or cutting from her own garden, to barter for a new rose or a brighter blossom of some sort, with which she would return in triumph. I fancied that sometimes she had to go by night on these charming quests. I could see her business-like, small figure setting forth down the steep path, when she had a good conscience toward her housekeeping and the children were in order to be left. I am sure that her friends thought of her when they were away from home and could bring her an offering of something rare. Alas, she had grown too old and feeble to care for her dear blossoms any longer, and had been forced to go to live with a married son. I dare say that she was thinking of her garden that very day, and wondering if this plant or that were not in bloom, and perhaps had a heartache at the thought that her tenants, the careless colored children, might tread the young shoots of peony and rose, and make havoc in the herb-bed. It was an uncommon collection, made by years of patient toil and self-sacrifice.

I thought of that deserted Southern garden as I followed my own New England road. The flower-plots were in gay bloom all along the way; almost every house had some flowers before it, sometimes carefully fenced about by stakes and barrel staves from the miscreant hens and chickens which lurked everywhere, and liked a good scratch and fluffing in soft earth this year as well as any other. The world seemed full of young life. There were calves tethered in pleasant shady spots, and puppies and kittens adventuring from the door-ways. The trees were full of birds: bobolinks, and cat-birds, and yellow-hammers, and golden robins, and sometimes a thrush, for the afternoon was wearing late. We passed the spring which famous spot in the early settlement of the country, but many of its old traditions are now forgotten. One of the omnipresent regicides of Charles the First is believed to have hidden himself for a long time under a great rock close by. The story runs that he made his miserable home in this den for several years, but I believe that there is no record that more than three of the regicides escaped to this country, and their wanderings are otherwise accounted for. There is a firm belief that one of them came to York, and was the ancestor of many persons now living there, but I do not know whether he can have been the hero of the Baker's Spring hermitage beside. We stopped to drink some of the delicious water, which never fails to flow cold and clear under the shade of a great oak, and were amused with the sight of a flock of gay little country children who passed by in deep conversation. What could such atoms of humanity be talking about? "Old times," said John, the master of horse, with instant decision.

We met now and then a man or woman, who stopped to give us hospitable greeting; but there was no staying for visits, lest the daylight might fail us. It was delightful to find this old-established neighborhood so thriving and populous, for a few days before I had driven over three miles of road, and passed only one house that was tenanted, and six cellars or crumbling chimneys where good farmhouses had been, the lilacs blooming in solitude, and the fields, cleared with so much difficulty a century or two ago, all going back to the original woodland from which they were won. What would the old farmers say to see the fate of their worthy bequest to the younger generation? They would wag their heads sorrowfully, with sad foreboding.

After we had passed more woodland and a well-known quarry, where, for a wonder, the derrick was not creaking and not a single hammer was clinking at the stone wedges, we did not see any one hoeing in the fields, as we had seen so many on the white rose road, the other side of the hills. Presently we met two or three people walking sedately, clad in their best clothes. There was a subdued air of public excitement and concern, and one of us remembered that there had been a death in the neighborhood; this was the day of the funeral. The man had been known to us in former years. We had an instinct to hide our unsympathetic pleasuring, but there was nothing to be done except to follow our homeward road straight by the house.

The occasion was nearly ended by this time: the borrowed chairs were being set out in the yard in little groups; even the funeral supper had been eaten, and the brothers and sisters and near relatives of the departed man were just going home. The new grave showed plainly out in the green field near by. He had belonged to one of the ancient families of the region, long settled on this old farm by the narrow river; they had given their name to a bridge, and the bridge had christened the meeting-house which stood close by. We were much struck by the solemn figure of the mother, a very old woman, as she walked toward her old home with some of her remaining children. I had not thought to see her again, knowing her great age and infirmity. She was like a presence out of the last century, tall and still erect, dark-eyed and of striking features, and a firm look not modern, but as if her mind were still set upon an earlier and simpler scheme of life. An air of dominion cloaked her finely. She had long been queen of her surroundings and law-giver to her great family. Royalty is a quality, one of Nature's gifts, and there one might behold it as truly as if Victoria Regina Imperatrix had passed by. The natural instincts common to humanity were there undisguised, unconcealed, simply accepted. We had seen a royal progress; she was the central figure of that rural society; as you looked at the little group, you could see her only. Now that she came abroad so rarely, her presence was not without deep significance, and so she took her homeward way with a primitive kind of majesty.

It was evident that the neighborhood was in great excitement and quite thrown out of its usual placidity. An acquaintance came from a small house farther down the road, and we stopped for a word with

SARAH ORNE JEWETT

him. We spoke of the funeral, and were told something of the man who had died. "Yes, and there's a man layin' very sick here," said our friend in an excited whisper. "He won't last but a day or two. There's another man buried yesterday that was struck by lightnin', comin' acrost a field when that great shower begun. The lightnin' stove through his hat and run down all over him, and ploughed a spot in the ground." There was a knot of people about the door; the minister of that scattered parish stood among them, and they all looked at us eagerly, as if we too might be carrying news of a fresh disaster through the countryside.

Somehow the melancholy tales did not touch our sympathies as they ought, and we could not see the pathetic side of them as at another time, the day was so full of cheer and the sky and earth so glorious. The very fields looked busy with their early summer growth, the horses began to think of the clack of the oat-bin cover, and we were hurried along between the silvery willows and the rustling alders, taking time to gather a handful of stray-away conserve roses by the roadside; and where the highway made a long bend eastward among the farms, two of us left the carriage, and followed a footpath along the green river bank and through the pastures, coming out to the road again only a minute later than the horses. I believe that it is an old Indian trail followed from the salmon falls farther down the river, where the up-country Indians came to dry the plentiful fish for their winter supplies. I have traced the greater part of this deep-worn footpath, which goes straight as an arrow across the country, the first day's trail being from the falls (where Mason's settlers came in 1627, and built their Great Works of a saw-mill with a gang of saws, and presently a grist mill beside) to Emery's Bridge. I should like to follow the old footpath still farther. I found part of it by accident a long time ago. Once, as you came close to the river, you were sure to find fishermen scattered along,—sometimes I myself have been discovered; but it is not much use to go fishing any more. If some public-spirited person would kindly be the Frank Buckland of New England, and try to have the laws enforced that protect the inland fisheries, he would do his country great service. Years ago, there were so many salmon that, as an enthusiastic old friend once assured me, "you could walk across on them below the falls;" but now they are unknown, simply because certain substances which would enrich the farms are thrown from factories and tanneries into our clear New England streams. Good river fish are growing very scarce. The smelts, and bass, and shad have all left this upper branch of the Piscataqua, as the salmon left it long ago, and the supply of one necessary sort of good cheap food is lost to a growing community, for the lack of a little thought and care in the factory companies and saw-mills, and the building in some cases of fish-ways over the dams. I think that the need of preaching against this bad economy is very great. The sight of a proud lad with a string of undersized trout will scatter half the idlers in town into the pastures next day, but everybody patiently accepts the depopulation of a fine clear river, where the tide comes fresh from the sea to be tainted by the spoiled stream, which started from its mountain sources as pure as heart could wish. Man has done his best to ruin the world he lives in, one is tempted to say at impulsive first thought; but after all, as I mounted the last hill before reaching the village, the houses took on a new look of comfort and pleasantness; the fields that I knew so well were a fresher green than before, the sun was down, and the provocations of the day seemed very slight compared to the satisfaction. I believed that with a little more time we should grow wiser about our fish and other things beside.

It will be good to remember the white rose road and its quietness in many a busy town day to come. As I think of these slight sketches, I wonder if they will have to others a tinge of sadness; but I have seldom spent an afternoon so full of pleasure and fresh and delighted consciousness of the possibilities of rural life.

CPSIA information can be obtained
at www.ICGtesting.com
Printed in the USA
BVHW091832240521
608028BV00012B/254

9 781513 279879